MORE SEX-I

When I discovered a love letter to my husband from another woman I was outraged. However, I have to admit its highly explicit content also turned me on. She described in detail the threesome she'd just had with her husband and mine, the pair of them obviously taking her to heaven and back – the slut. At first I wanted to scratch her eyes out – then I just felt envious. And so horny I couldn't help putting my hand up my skirt.

When my husband got home later, I confronted him and Greg swore it had just been a one-off. He said he'd gone home for a drink with Ken, a workmate, but the pair of them had ended up watching a porno video with Ken's wife, Lauren. And one thing, as they say, had led to another.

Greg asked if I could forgive him and I said yes – on one condition. I'd always fancied having two men at the same time . . .

Elaine T., Essex

Also available from Headline:

Passion Beach
Playing the Field
Room Service
Sin and Mrs Saxon
The Depravities of Marisa Bond
The Finishing School
Treasure Hunt
The Exhibitionists
The Casting Couch
Masque of Flesh
Indecent Display
Naked Ambition
Cremorne Gardens
Eroticon Dreams
What Katy Dunn Did
The Wife-Watcher Letters
The Delta Sex-Life Letters
Dangerous Desires
Amorous Appetites
A Man with Three Maids
Saucy Habits
Empire of Lust
The Lusts of the Borgias

More Sex-Life Letters

Edited and compiled by
Lesley Asquith

Delta

Publisher's message
This novel creates an imaginary sexual world. In the real world, readers are advised to practise safe sex.

First published in 1999
by HEADLINE BOOK PUBLISHING

A HEADLINE DELTA paperback

10 9 8 7 6 5 4 3 2

ISBN 0 7472 6035 4

Typeset by Avon Dataset Ltd, Bidford-on-Avon, Warks

Printed and bound in Great Britain by
Mackays of Chatham PLC, Chatham, Kent

HEADLINE BOOK PUBLISHING
A division of Hodder Headline PLC
338 Euston Road,
London NW1 3BH

www.headline.co.uk
www.hodderheadline.co.uk

More Sex-Life Letters

INTRODUCTION

When I first appealed some years ago for letters on the subject of sexual experience I was overwhelmed by a tide of graphic and detailed stories. The result was the publication of *The Delta Sex-Life Letters*.

Such was the continuing interest shown by my correspondents that I have prepared this further volume in the series, whose contents are no less explicit.

Once again thanks are due to all those lusty spirits out there, male and female, young and mature, who are eager to share their erotic experiences. Good luck to you all and may I add – as many of them have added to me – 'Keep up the good work!'

Lesley Asquith, London 1999

1. Please Please Me

Playing Away
Two Into One
In Praise of Other Women
Mother Came Too
Long-Distance Lust
Oral Tributes
Fair Exchange
Neighbourhood Watch
Only Make-Believe
Family Welcome
Loose Talk
Blue Moves

Playing Away

My husband is not greatly interested in sex, although he's a loving partner in every other way and a good father. I do not want to break with him or leave our two sons and teenage daughter, so I seek outside sexual relationships. It is not difficult to find a willing partner – I can always 'turn on' or be 'turned on' by other men. My rule for these liaisons is to make it plain any sexual affair remain purely physical and for the sole object of having satisfying sex. Over the twenty years of marriage I have had no difficulty sticking to this rule in all cases but one.

That was an affair with a colleague at a private school where I was teaching. He was young, handsome, full of life, and at a dull period of my life I fell heavily in love with him. This was only the second affair I'd had. The first was with a family friend; his wife and I were cousins. When he kissed me in his car the first time, it was not the passion of his kiss but the idea I was allowing something so wicked that turned me on. We met for sex both at his home and mine when the opportunity arose, and we also fucked in his car at times.

He was no great lover. He was strictly a 'put it in and waggle it about' type and if he made me climax it was because I'm always ready to come if aroused. A kiss or two before removing my knickers was the extent of foreplay between us, but I thought that was normal as that was how my husband and I made love.

In this second affair with the young teacher, I learned how different sex could be and how much more varied and exciting it was with an experienced lover. Simon was oversexed and quite shameless. He insisted I strip naked the first time I visited his flat, and used his tongue in my mouth and in my vagina to excite me, something I immediately loved, as I did the crude words he used during sex.

He talked of fucking my face and breasts, and did so with relish frequently during our affair. I was always made to swallow his come unless he wanted to shoot it over my face or breasts. Every position possible was used during sex, or fucking as he insisted I call it, ordering me to use the terms prick, cunt and arse during the height of our lovemaking. He preferred me on my elbows and knees when fucking me, and was as often up my back passage as my cunt. I found his dominating attitude heightened my arousal and I behaved as if I was his slave.

The fact I was being unfaithful was, and still is, one of the pleasures of having an affair. With Simon having me even in our lunch break at school, and in his car after school, I'd go home to husband and family with a glow of wicked pride at what I was doing. I considered I was still a good wife, as I performed a wife's duties as well as ever. Being shared by two men has always been something I've enjoyed. As I say, apart from falling for Simon, all my other affairs have been purely physical. A reminder of that love is my youngest son, as I broke a rule and allowed myself to be made pregnant by Simon. My husband has no inkling that the boy is not his. I'm sure he's not the only husband unaware that one of his children is not of his making. Only the mother knows for certain, after all.

With other lovers (there have been seven over the years), I encourage them to be as macho as Simon. Those that are not, I dump, as I can get that kind of loving at home. Each lover has been different, with different desires. One liked to prepare for each sex session by lightly spanking me over his knee. One was into taking photos of me naked and in erotic positions as I pleasured myself with sex toys. Another insisted on paying me after each meeting at an hotel – playing the part of a prostitute was an added thrill.

My latest love is a policeman who came to give a road safety lecture at my present school. During coffee in the staff room, our eyes met and we both *knew*. That's how it is. He's perfect: highly sexed, big built, and does not intend to leave his wife – which has been a danger with some men. Sometimes when I'm with him and feel broody, I want to have his child. It's a desire I'm finding harder to resist, so who knows? I've got away with it once and know I could again. Last time, being helped out of the bath by my husband with my belly hugely rounded, I could see him swell with pride. I'm sure he'd feel the same way again.

Lisa, Paisley

Two Into One

I left my wife years ago because her idea of marital sex was for me to do a Santa Claus and come once a year. Stuff that, I thought. The divorce cost me a bundle but it's been worth every penny as I'm free to fuck my brains out around the world with willing women like Maria, an unattached Irish girl I met on holiday in Florida.

The fact I was twice her age didn't stop her sleeping with me the first day we met. We hit it off at a scuba-diving session. I took her to dinner and then we fucked and sucked all night in my hotel room. I was hard-put to keep up with this sex-greedy lady but with my dick, mouth and fingers all brought into play she had no complaints. Tall and statuesque, with flame-red hair and milk-white tits, her hungry cunt couldn't get enough of my thrusting dick.

Soon she moved into my room and the hotel staff began to refer to her as my wife. I wasn't in the market for marriage but I was proud they thought I was the husband of such a sexy beauty. She used to come in loud shuddering spasms, having multiple climaxes on my dick in every position, and loved to have her mouth and tits fucked too. She teased me that I couldn't do better than marry her, we had so much in common as well as a love of sex. Secretly I was inclined to agree with her but had no intention of getting hitched again.

She was everything I looked for in a woman: randy as hell and completely uninhibited. She walked around the room naked, just begging to be fondled and fucked. Back in England she was a member of a nudist group, something I'd always longed to try. I thought how different she was from my ex-wife, who would never dream of asking for a fuck. I'd be watching TV when Maria would kneel between my legs and give me a loving sucking off. Something else she liked to do was to discuss screwing around. It was highly arousing erotic talk to listen to.

She told me her favourite fantasy was to be fucked by two big black hunks. As it happened, a pair of friendly cops patrolled the area of our hotel, both huge ebony-coloured guys. Off duty, they would come into the hotel bar and one night I joined them for drinks. Talk got around to sexual matters and I invited them up to my room. There it seemed we accidently caught Maria in her bathrobe, about to shower before dinner. The two men saw what was on offer, telling me what a gorgeous wife I had while shrewdly guessing why they'd been invited up.

Right away, one insisted that Maria show them her big tits, the deep cleavage and creamy upper slopes already revealed by the open neck of her robe. To make sure she was indeed a willing subject, I warned her that the cops fancied her and fully intended to fuck her. 'That's right, ma'am,' said the one called Ben. 'It's what we're good at.' Maria laughed and said 'Promises, promises.' As if challenged, both men stripped off and began stroking massive ebony cocks before her. 'Hey,' Maria enthused, 'these two weren't at the back of the line when pricks were handed out.'

You could say that again, I thought, seeing the size of their full erections. Both lads were into body-building or weight-lifting, fine physical specimens of manhood that I could see Maria appreciated. She slipped the robe from her shoulders and cheekily wobbled her bare tits under their noses. All she wore was a pair of pretty little lace panties, the dark triangle of hair on her cunt bulge showing through.

She fell back across the bed, peeling off the panties and tossing them at me, laughing as they landed on my head. 'If you can't bear to see me being fucked by these two studs, Robert,' she cried out, 'you'd better leave the room now.' To the pair of horny cops standing by, she said, 'You are going to fuck me, aren't you, boys?' The older patrolman, Calvin, assured her they would. Parting her thighs and lowering his face, he began tracing his tongue up and down the swollen lips of her pouting quim.

Soon she was moaning and writhing in pleasure, begging for someone to give her a cock. She got one, thick as my wrist and black as ebony as Ben knelt on the bed beside her head, grasping her hair to twist her face around. The randy cow parted her lips as Ben fed his monster of a tool into her mouth, telling her to *suck, baby, suck* and I saw her cheeks hollowing as she suctioned the big stalk avidly. Between her spreadeagled thighs Calvin's tongue was delving deep into her hot moist channel. As he licked, nipped and sucked her clitty, her moans of pleasure issued through a mouthful of stiff prick.

The pair of lusty cops worked on her until the scent of highly excited cunt filled the room. My prick was as hard as blue steel seeing the going-over she was getting, but I also felt a bitter-sweet resentment that the visitors were making free with *my* woman and she, the dirty slut, was loving it so much. Then Calvin ceased tonguing her cunt and hoisted her legs over his shoulders, thrusting into her. The feel of his huge throbber buried to the hilt in her love-tube made her buck and jerk as she still sucked greedily on Ben's big dick.

'Go on, fuck the whore rigid!' I shouted, annoyed they were making her so excited. 'Screw the arse off the dirty bitch!' But it struck me while shouting abuse and watching her being filled by cock at both ends that Maria was the kind of slut that suited me. I reminded myself that though she liked to fuck with other men it was arousing to watch, and with her there was plenty to go around.

'My turn to slip her a length,' Ben informed his mate, pulling his big purple knob from Maria's mouth. As Calvin withdrew his limp dick after emptying his balls into her steaming pussy, Ben flipped her over. She now lay on her elbows and knees; her mouth still open, ready for more cock. She complained about both pricks being taken out of her, getting a flurry of hard smacks on her raised bum for being so impatient.

'Oh, yes! Spank me, warm my bottom good!' the randy Maria yelled. Pinned down arse up, with Ben curled over her back, he used his strength to prise her buttock cheeks wide apart. With his pole-like prick going in between the cushiony cleave of her bottom, she tilted her rear as if offering herself for penetration. Calvin, not to be left out of things, got on the bed and squatted before her face. With one hand he gripped her hair and with the other he rubbed his flaccid cock over her lips, ordering her to suck him hard.

'Yeah, I'll stretch her ass, you stretch her mouth,' Ben said to his mate. Once she'd taken it in the rear, Mary groaned as if in agony, but it was an agony of lust and she urged him on. Looking at me with dazed eyes, she grunted that his enormous cock was thudding into her like a pile-driver, but it was *good*, absolute heaven to be filled so full. Fucked by big thrusting pricks both fore and aft, Maria was in ecstasy, out of control and hardly aware whether she was coming or going.

The two cops left after making her lick clean every inch of their saturated knobs. I felt enough was enough as they stood beside the bed while Maria kneeled up with a dick in each hand, cleaning both with her tongue. 'That's my wife you're making suck your big black pricks,' I complained. 'Aren't the pair of you content with fucking her?' Maria told me not to be so possessive and, when they'd gone, suggested I get on the bed and fuck her. With a while to kill before dinner, we had the horniest fucking session I'd ever known.

Maria came time after time, my prick a steel ramrod inside her. Afterwards we lay recovering and she teased me that it had been so good because I'd watched the two cops having her 'everywhere' as she put it. I knew that was true. Then she reminded me I'd called out that it was my wife being made to lick clean their cocks. 'If you feel that way about me,' she smiled, 'why not make it real? Marry me and it *will* be your wife you'll enjoy seeing other men fuck.' That was a proposal I couldn't turn down and what we did on our honeymoon is another story!

Robert, Isle of Wight

In Praise of Other Women

I'm glad to announce I'm a lesbian. My love life is entirely fulfilling without men but I didn't discover my real preferences until I had had several male partners.

These turned out to be dismal failures. At a loose end, I went on holiday with an older woman who taught at the same school as I. We shared a room. One day, after exploring the lower slopes of the Swiss Alps, she seduced me in the shower on our return. Perhaps I do her a great injustice for I was more than keen to be taken to bed by her. I adored her mature body with its full breasts and strapping thighs. At first I was shocked by what we were doing and the fact I was finding it so pleasurable, but such was her tenderness and her concern for my feelings that I knew it was right.

For those two weeks we slept nude together and I discovered the delights of female lovemaking. The torrid sex we enjoyed was out of this world. I'd always admired Marion, but now I worshipped her. I wanted to devour her and was unable to wait until nightfall for us to make love. I soon learned what she liked and what I liked too. During the day I loved to have her loll back on the bed, legs hanging over the edge so I could kneel between her thighs to feast on her delicious quim. Often we did the same to each other with our bodies reversed in the 69 position.

On our return home, Marion accepted a headmistress's post in Devon, but before leaving we had nights out together which introduced me to the haunts of others who shared our style of loving. I attended parties with a happy crowd of women, all having naughty fun and games without shame. I found shaven pubes were favoured, not just for hygienic reasons but genital kissing and tonguing was considered nicer on smooth bare pubic lips. I was shaved by my new friends and, like them, expected to present a 'shaven haven' at our regular get-togethers.

These meetings were much looked forward to. With Marion in Devon, I wickedly played the field, getting quite a name for being a flirt. We'd openly have sex in public. Games like truth or forfeits were popular, and being bent over a female knee for a fun spanking was a frequent occurence. I was introduced to the use of dildoes and vibrators and felt no embarrassment at having them used on me or using such devices on other girls. I say 'girls', but our ages ranged from eighteen to the fifties, all of us in a room completely naked. As I was young and petite, I was often made to sit on the older women's laps and suck on their nipples, which I liked.

I was very much a 'fem' as girlish lesbians are called, that is the passive type, willing to obey a strict mistress. This was observed by the others of our group and by one woman especially, who was a newcomer and who began to pay particular attention to me. Barbara was well-built and attractive in a mannish way. She made it plain that I was her property. Though I was flattered by this, I still wanted to play the flirt but she told me that this she could not allow.

It was exciting to think someone felt that way about me and, being the passive kind of lesbian, I was attracted to her. I was invited to her flat for dinner, and I displeased her by saying I would not be hers exclusively. She ordered me to strip and then caned my bottom for my defiance. Later I was tied to her bed with soft cords and she made love to me in a way that became our favourite. Barbara would lie on top of me like a man, our breasts rubbing together, and our vaginal lips and clitorises in direct contact. She would then increase the pressure on our pubic regions and move backwards and forwards in a shunting motion which pressed our sensitive sexual parts together enticingly.

Soon both of us would be on fire with lust, our quims moist and slippery, ending in powerful orgasms that could be continued until both of us were sated. Following such bouts with Barbara, I was invariably ordered to lick her body clean, known to her as a 'tongue bath' and with loving attention demanded in the thorough cleansing of her sodden sex. Needless to say I was willingly 'forced' into being Barbara's slave and performing these acts. I loved being made to obey her every whim, even the smackings and canings that the least disobedience earned me.

There were other loving moments when passionate kissing, breast fondling and sucking, body contact, penetration of our vaginas by fingers or vibrators and prolonged oral sex was mutual. At these times I did not have to 'pretend' to refuse my mistress and be 'taken' by her. This was when she felt loving towards me and would ask if I truly loved her and would promise not to be cruel to me again. Of course she was when the mood took her (or when I craved being dominated) and being bound, caned and 'raped' was as much a source of sexual excitement to me as it was to her. Never did I agree to anything that I didn't want. Unlike many men, Barbara had true sexual imagination.

I believe there are more secret or would-be lesbians out there than men would dream of. Even married women ponder the advantages of having a same-sex lover. There's no risk of pregnancy for a start. I know one of our group advertises herself as a masseuse for ladies who like private attention at home. My friend's advertising slogan is 'Have oils, will travel' and her phone is always busy. She tells me most female clients employ her regularly for relief of sexual tension. These are married women who are not getting marital satisfaction. They enjoy exposing their bodies to one of their own kind and relax under the masseuse's soft feminine hands.

Usually, after a second visit, they permit more intimate fondling, doing whatever the masseuse suggests until full lesbian sex is enjoyed. Hubby doesn't suspect a thing – and he usually picks up the bill.

Carla, Manchester

Mother Came Too

I had always claimed I wasn't possessive of my big-titted, broad-arsed young wife. May was never short of lecherous glances from admiring men but, as far as I knew, she had never been unfaithful, although no doubt she had had offers.

My job involved travelling, which gave me scope for regular one-night stands. Then May found a lurid letter from a hotel receptionist I fucked whenever I stayed at her hotel (which saved me booking a room by sleeping with her instead). Surprisingly, my wife accepted that travelling all over for my work led to me being tempted. Shc forgave me without anger and, when getting aroused during foreplay, wanted to know all the lurid details of my screwing around. I liked recounting them because it made us horny as hell.

There was no doubt that being told all the facts of screwing other women turned my wife on tremendously. Well, I wasn't complaining as it certainly got her hot. A good wife and mother, she had never refused me sex and often made the advances, cuddling into me and telling me to fuck her. There wasn't a place in the house we hadn't screwed, even in the bath or the kitchen for a 'table-ender' among the breakfast dishes when the kids were staying with my mother.

Last summer we went to Jersey for two weeks holiday. We rented a cottage and took my mother who had been widowed two years before. The weather was great and we spent hours on the beach with the kids and in the sea. May looked a voluptuous picture in her bikini and my mother felt in the mood and asked if she could borrow May's spare bikini. I wasn't too happy about this, for my mother was generously endowed. However, if you're into big tits and rounded arse cheeks, she is your kind of lady.

One morning I took the two little ones to a children's park while my wife and mother went to the beach to swim and sunbathe. After an hour or two of amusing the kids on the swings and roundabouts, we went back to the beach to rejoin May and my mum. As I approached I saw that two men were sitting with them on the sand. Both were young and wearing the briefest of bathing trunks. They stood up as I got nearer, showing off swimming pouches that bulged with their cocks and balls. Excusing themselves, they walked off, going past me without so much as a glance.

Both my wife and mother were showing lots of tit, the way their large breasts overflowed the bikini bra cups. Down below mere triangles of material covered their pubic areas. Seeing me frown, and I'm talking about me who'd had so many fucks on the side and boasted to his wife about them, both women began teasing me that they could still attract good-looking men. The two were German tourists and had stopped in passing to chat them up, declaring they were sisters which pleased my mother no end.

Later, back at the cottage, my wife taunted me that my jealousy was showing. It was true and I hated myself for resenting that the two German blokes wanted to fuck both women. I should have understood that as, after all, I never caught sight of a good-looking bird without wanting to screw her. However, I found it was different when it involved your own kind. To make up for being surly, I agreed to baby-sit that night. There was a dinner-dance followed by a cabaret at a local hotel which my mother wished to attend, with my wife for company. My mum being widowed and a regular baby-sitter for May and me, I could hardly refuse.

When the pair left to go to the hotel by taxi, almost at once a furious summer storm began. The rain thundered down in torrents and the electricity failed. It was next morning before my wife and mother returned, explaining the roads had been flooded and no taxis had been able to operate. It was not until we were home from the holiday months later that the truth came out. May and I were fondling each other in bed, working ourselves up with randy talk about my past conquests when she suddenly went into a fit of giggles. Intrigued, I asked her what was so amusing.

'Can you stand hearing it?' she challenged. And I learned for the first time about the stormy night on holiday. The German guys had told my wife and mother about the dinner-dance at their hotel and invited them. They had been wined and dined and thoroughly enjoyed themselves on the dancefloor until the German lads had asked them up to their bedroom. I lay trying to conceal my rising jealousy as May went on. 'Why didn't you refuse to go?' I said moodily.

'Ask your ma,' May said. 'She'd told me earlier that since she was a widow and not getting any, she wasn't going to refuse if one of the boys made a move on her.' While I was digesting this information, my wife carried on telling me what had transpired in the bedroom. With the lights failing, candles had illuminated the room, which added to the romantic atmosphere. At first May had kept her partner at arm's length, but just a few feet away on the other single bed, my mother was engaged in a torrid snog with her bloke. It was thrilling to watch them, May said, especially when they removed their clothes and he began to fuck her. 'Your mother's moans of satisfaction turned me on,' she said. 'What else could I do? The guy soon got me across the bed and out of my clothes. I couldn't help myself.'

I could picture the scene. The hotel bedroom lit by candleglow and reeking of sex. On the single beds the two women closest to me lying naked, being vigorously penetrated by two lusty lovers. As May went on, describing every lewd bit of information about the session, I learned that both men had been expert at making the women come by tonguing their cunts. Worse, as the night proceeded, with fucking and sucking continuing into the dawn, the men had changed partners, having both women in turn.

It all became too much for me. Telling her to stop, May smiled and reminded me that I'd had no qualms about regaling her with my sex exploits. 'I thought you'd enjoy hearing my side for once,' she said. But I didn't enjoy it much. Sometimes ignorance is bliss.

Rory, Carlisle

Long-Distance Lust

I've no doubt that adult phone lines are a con but after my recent experiences I can see why they appeal to some people. In my work as an executive's secretary I was on the phone all the time. One business manager I used to call was friendly, chatty, nicely spoken. I never met him as he lived at the other end of the country and had no real reason to visit our office.

Once, in the middle of an emergency deal, he had to call my home number in the evening to verify something. Then I left the firm and worked elsewhere. A year or so went by until one evening, alone at home and lonely after breaking up with my boyfriend, I got a call from my businessman friend. He said he was sitting at home and suddenly remembered me, so having nothing else to do decided he would give me a call to see how I was. I was already tearful, so I told him I was sad because my live-in lover had moved out and left me.

'More fool him,' my friend at the other end of the line said. 'I've never met you, of course, but your voice sounds so husky and sexy I've always pictured you as a voluptuous blonde. Am I right, Miss Lane?'

'Something like that,' I admitted, for I am fair and what you might call pleasantly plump. As our talk continued we got on the subject of sex and how much we missed it. He was divorced and said he found satisfaction in masturbating. Did I pleasure myself? he asked. Shocked, but finding myself getting excited, I murmured shyly that I did. He made me repeat myself and I found myself boldly admitting that I played with myself.

'Do it now while we talk,' he said suddenly, his voice sounding different as his excitement mounted. 'Do it and tell me what you're doing while I rub myself up. Don't be shy.'

It occurred to me I'd got a pervert on the line, but my own arousal prevented me banging the phone down. At first I invented what I was doing, saying I'd pulled down my knickers and, with legs apart, lying back in my armchair, I was fingering myself off. From his end the groans and gasps told me he was bringing himself off. I began to make similar sounds into the receiver to make him think that I was coming too. After he'd recovered, his breathing still short, he thanked me and said it was the best orgasm he'd ever had. Then he hung up.

I was shaking, thrilled to think I was the cause of his extreme pleasure. Roused so unusually, I then did what I'd told him I'd been doing. I slipped down my briefs and fingered myself, thinking back on our lewd phone call. Almost at once I began to spasm in an orgasm that went on and on, only later realising that such was my arousal I'd given myself multiple climaxes, the first I'd experienced. As I lay recovering I secretly wished that my long-distance lover would call again.

He did and, over the next few telephone conversations, 'seduced' me into doing whatever he cared to suggest. I was made to lie naked along the settee in my living room while receiving his instructions or answering leading questions about my sex life. Soon we became totally uninhibited in our talk and actions, and I was saying and doing things that I would never have dreamed of.

In time we became very creative in making up the lewdest stories about our past sex experiences. These became weirder and wilder in our attempts to give ourselves noisy, long-distance climaxes.

We all have sexual fantasies, no doubt, but most of them remain secret. I found it highly erotic to confess them to someone else, especially when it made my listener so horny. I told him how I allowed boyfriends to spank me, titty-fuck my breasts and have anal sex. For his benefit I pretended I'd sucked off a whole rugby team in their coach, and made love to other women in a wild lesbian romp that was videoed by my then boyfriend. Often we came off together while talking over the telephone. I found it very exciting when, in his throes, my phone partner called me names and said, 'You'd let anyone fuck you, you sexy slut.'

Now I have a new boyfriend, a nice man who finds me attractive and treats me like a lady. In time he may ask me to be his wife. My worry is how he'll react when he finds out what I'm really like with my knickers off. Will he give me all the wild fucking I really want? Or shall I be reaching for the telephone?

Joan L., Croydon

Oral Tributes

My wife has always derived a great deal of pleasure from the act of sucking me off, loving the taste and feel of a stiff cock in her mouth. Unfortunately, I discovered it wasn't only my cock that she enjoyed in her mouth. There'd been quite a few, in fact, and when I challenged her about it she claimed oral sex wasn't really being unfaithful. Nobody else had fucked her, she said, and that's what she considered adulterous. What can you do with such a woman?

In my case, stick with her. Though she'd been tempted and sucked other men's cocks, who was I to complain? She'd caught me out twice before. The first time was with her own sister who'd left her husband after a row and came to stay with us. Marje was supposed to be out shopping but, suspecting something, came back in the house and caught me screwing her sister on the couch. She said what annoyed her was that we'd gone behind her back. Knowing her sister Cheryl was doing without, Marje said she would have agreed if she'd asked to be fucked by me to keep her going.

Not many wives are as sympathetic as that, so I knew I had a good one. Soon after I learned that Marje enjoyed watching her sister and I screwing, joining in to make a threesome more often than not. To loll back and have two sisters bollock naked each side of you to fuck in turn, to have both sucking your dick to revive it for more shagging, makes forgiving a wife's lapses much easier.

And, as she pointed out to me, it was my fault that she had an insatiable appetite for fellatio, to use its posh term.

For we met as teenagers and it was I who cajoled and begged Marje to suck on my stalk. It had been done a few times to me by a married woman next door which gave me a great letch for the act. I don't want to go into male power and stuff, but it does boost the ego for a bloke to stand legs apart and feet planted looking down at the head of a female sucking you off. And when I started taking Marje out a grope and suck at her bare titties and even a feel at her quim was allowed, but she drew the line at letting me penetrate her.

So I kept on to her about sucking me off, showing willingness on my part by licking her out, something that made her go bananas with my tongue embedded in her quim, giving her repeated comes. Reluctant, but not wanting to lose me, she advanced to kissing the knob of my dick, flicking it with her tongue and tasting it. I saw by the way she licked her lips that she enjoyed the taste. It was one trip to the cinema on a pouring wet night, when we were the only people at the rear of the balcony, that finally made her discover she loved it.

We'd been fondling and kissing, unaware of what was being screened, when she unzipped me and brought out my dick. Of course it was hard, hot and sticky in her grasp, and I noted that she couldn't help stopping wanking me to take her fingers to her lips. She was unable to resist the taste, I reckoned, so I suggested to her how nicer it would be to have the source of the taste she evidently enjoyed inside her mouth. To suck on and savour the flavour, sort of thing, not mentioning of course. I was angling to have her suck me off at last.

No doubt highly aroused, plus the wicked thought of

doing it in a public place, to my joy Marje was helpless to stop herself sinking to the floor with her head between my legs. A few tentative sucks, and she was a goner, loving the feel of rigid flesh on her tongue. Her cheeks hollowing, head bobbing, she began to give me a lovely gobble. Even when a couple of arrivals were shown into seats a few rows ahead of us, Marje did not stop, greedy to suck my balls empty of hot jism. After that it was the done thing, sucking me off whenever the chance offered, the rear seat of my car witness to regular blow-jobs but no fucking until we married.

It was some years later that I caught her in the hotel room of a lad we'd met on holiday. A football player in one of the lower divisions, he was there with his girlfriend. She was by herself at the pool one afternoon when I returned from a fishing trip. With no Marje there and the girlfriend sunning herself alone, a niggling suspicion made me go into the hotel to look for her.

Looking in on the other room, I saw the bloke lying back on his elbows on the bed, his spread legs over the edge. Kneeling in front of him, Marje was sucking avidly on his huge dong. I found the sight undoubtedly arousing. I turned away and when I charged her with it later, she admitted she'd been unable to resist sucking on such a big one. She excused herself by saying that though the chap had wanted to fuck her she'd made him settle for a blow-job. In time I was shown her diary, with details of many secret suckings recorded there, including a few testaments to her expertise written in other's hands. She should be an expert – she gets enough practice. And I'm the lucky fellow she practises on.

Dougie, Inverness

Fair Exchange

When I discovered an extremely explicit love letter to my husband from a married woman I knew, I was shocked. However, its lurid content also turned me on. In it, the woman described the threesome she had evidently enjoyed with her husband and *mine*, fucking and sucking her to climax after climax. I cursed her at first, then was made terribly horny reading how both men had given her the sexual experience of her life. At first I wanted to scratch her eyes out, then I felt real envy for her in trying out what had been a secret fantasy of mine – to be bedded by two randy males and fucked out of my mind.

The more I thought about it, the randier I became. Lolling back in an armchair and still holding the letter, my hand went under my skirt and rubbed hard against my crotch. Anyone glancing in the window would have seen me helplessly jerking my bottom from the seat as I came violently in seconds. That's how aroused the thought of having two men at a time had got me, leaving me drained by the strength of the climax. I found the gusset of my panties soaked, wet from the copious lubrication of my arousal.

The letter had got a little soggy too, from the hectic contact with my excited quim. When my husband, Greg, came home later, and I confronted him, he stuttered apologies and promised it had just been a one-off. Ken was a workmate who had invited Greg home after an hour or two overtime at their office. My husband swore he thought it was just to have a drink, but Ken and his wife, Lauren, put on a porno video featuring a threesome. Soon they were all made randy, that when Ken said he and his wife were into threesomes, my Greg couldn't help joining in.

I had to concede that it would have been impossible for any man, especially my randy hubby. Asking if he'd been forgiven, I told him only if he allowed me the same pleasure – to be bedded by two men at the same time. I wanted all the things done to me that Lauren had enjoyed. Her husband Ken was a handsome big lad a few years younger than me, and obviously virile. He would do fine to make up a threesome, I told Greg, otherwise I'm going round to their house and I'll make such a scene everyone will learn what has been going on.

My husband was not keen on having Ken or anyone else fucking me despite what he'd been up to! How like a man. When I repeated that I *would* cause a scandal, he knew he had to comply. He spoke to Ken, grumpily telling me that Ken had seemed only too bloody eager to join in a threesome with me. It's my turn now, I told Greg, pointing out that the letter I'd found had been an invitation to continue meeting Ken and Lauren. I bet you'd have been back for more, I charged him. I had no doubt about it, especially as the horny slut had written at length how good it had been with my husband's tongue licking out her cunt; how she had loved what he did to her tits (no prizes for guessing), and that his prick had felt so big and hard when plunging inside her greedy quim.

The next day my phone rang and I picked it up to hear Ken at the other end. He thought I must be a sex maniac to make my husband arrange a threesome, so right away he was rude and crude as he spoke to me. 'Always fancied fucking you, Elaine,' were almost his first words after saying how Greg had invited him to share me and how he'd jumped at the chance. 'I can't wait to see your big tits and arse and have you begging for the cock. We'll have a ball. Do you suck prick? You'd better be prepared to do the lot.'

When the evening came, I found myself immediately stripped naked while being kissed and fondled by two randy men. It was thrilling to be manhandled by such eager lovers, both with huge cockstands rearing in anticipation. As I parted my thighs and stroked my cunt lips in invitation, both fondled my tits and I felt a greedy mouth clamped to each nipple. I closed my eyes deliberately so that it became a game guessing who was doing what to me. A finger wanked me for a while, diddling my wet inner flesh and circling my clitty. Groaning my pleasure, my hips writhed and arse bucked as the ecstasy mounted.

'One of you fuck me!' I cried out and heard Ken order me not to be impatient. Then I felt a mouth slide over my pulsating fanny and a tongue giving me a superb licking out. I came in a frenzy and even while in the throes heard my husband's voice saying, 'Flip her over and fuck her from the rear, it's what the dirty bitch likes.'

'Yes, yes, fuck me from behind,' I eagerly responded, and Ken laughed and said I was a regular little horny slut, a real cock-lover. He added that I'd no doubt taken a good few pricks in my time. 'No doubt the cow has,' I heard my husband agree and he delivered four or five good hard slaps to my bare bottom at the thought of me being a loose woman.

I felt Ken's belly press against my buttock cheeks,

his hands prising the cheeks apart and then the velvety knob of his cock slide between my pussy lips. Rearing my bum back to him as he lunged forward, every thick inch of his rigid stalk entered me, making me gasp aloud in pleasure. 'Fuck the horny cow senseless,' I heard my husband urge Ken, no doubt by now finding it arousing and highly erotic to see another man shafting me while I responded helplessly.

I too found it magically erotic hearing my own husband telling a man to fuck me, even delighting in being called names like slut and horny cow. No sooner had I had a second orgasm than Ken was groaning his lust as he jerked and shot his load into me. Greg was on me like a flash, his prick buried deep between my bottom cheeks and his hands around me, gripping my breasts to help him lunge into me. Not to be left out, even with his cock limp from fucking me, Ken got on the bed and squatted before my face. It was obvious what he wanted me to do, and I did it!

Sucking greedily on Ken's droopy dick soon had it growing long and thick between my tongue and palate. All the better to fuck me with again, I thought wantonly as, from behind, my eager hubby shafted me with enormous strength, driving into my soaking cunt like a relentless piston. In turn I buffeted his belly with my gyrating bottom, groaning and urging him on, tilting my arse and feeling him getting deeper in with every thrust. Spunked at both ends, it was but the start of a night of lustful sex that demonstrated to me that two men are certainly better than one to satisfy a lady.

Soon it was a once-weekly threesome between us, and I was sure my two randy males were doing the same for Ken's wife, Lauren. It was so good being serviced by

Greg and Ken that I couldn't blame Lauren for wanting the same. When we meet in the street or in the supermarket, we nod recognition as we pass. I'm tempted to tell her she's not the only one who is into threesome sex. It might be fun to compare notes!

Elaine T., Essex

Neighbourhood Watch

I hated my paper round because it meant dragging myself out of bed hours before school. But one day it went from being barely tolerable to becoming no problem at all. The reason for this was the voluptuous Mrs Beverley T.

The morning began as usual. Cleaning teeth, splashing a few droplets of water over my face, then into the kitchen to make tea and toast before cycling off to the newsagents. I let my mother have a lie-in as she worked late at a pub as a barmaid, dad having left us without means of support. I was filling the kettle at the kitchen sink under the window when I glanced out into the darkness.

The kitchen overlooked a tiny garden which backed on to another council flat opposite ours. In effect I was looking across about fifty yards of space when a light was switched on in an identical kitchen to the one I was in. As the kitchen was flooded with light I saw a woman in a nightdress walk to the sink under her window.

Fascinated, I stared as she peeled the cotton nightie over her head, revealing herself naked to the waist. She turned on the hot tap and began to wash herself at the sink. I knew the woman by sight, she was a single mum who drove a taxi and was considered a tough cookie.

I also knew her kids, went to school with them, knew they were bright. They were clean, warmly dressed and obviously well fed. Mrs T was admirably built. Although a mere lad, I'd ogled her curvy shape with lustful thoughts, especially her marvellous big teats which bobbed and bounced with her slightest movement.

I wasn't the only lad who thought that; remarks were made by other boys when Mrs T delivered her younger kids to school. Her tits were magnificent specimens: big, bulging, trembly and tilted, the contours perfection for the dedicated tit-lover. And now I was seeing them uncovered, in their full wobbly glory. She began washing her upper torso energetically.

Fearful of being seen, I retreated into the kitchen away from the window, then had the inspiration to switch off the light so that I could watch without being spotted. Her tits swung from side to side as she washed under her arms then dried herself. Finally she turned round and walked back to the door. This was good too as she wore the tiniest of brief knickers and I got a good view of her plump arse cheeks.

This happy state of affairs continued for the whole of that winter, making getting up worthwhile. As soon as Mrs T came into her kitchen and put on the light, off would go mine. I'd then settle with my nose against the window to enjoy the sight of her big tits being soaped and dried. I borrowed binoculars to magnify the view, never tiring of peeping on her until the mornings lightened.

For a while that summer she sunbathed in her tiny garden wearing a bikini that left little to the imagination. By the following winter she'd moved. Some years later, now in the army and on leave, I called a taxi from a pub late one night. To my surprise it was Mrs T who answered the call. 'I know you,' she said right away and with what I thought was a knowing smile. 'You're the boy who used to live opposite me when I stayed in the flats.'

I admitted that, and she laughed and asked if I'd enjoyed watching her washing at the sink? As she seemed to find it amusing and wasn't annoyed, I joked that there had been two good reasons for my early morning viewing. 'As soon as you put your kitchen light out I knew you were getting an eyeful of my tits,' she laughed. The upshot was after some chat, I got her to drive me to a curry house and get a takeaway followed by picking up some booze at the off-licence.

'Here, you're not too young for this?' she said later, on the couch at her house with those glorious tits now freed from blouse and bra and being actually fondled, kissed and sucked by me who had long admired them from a distance. The final and most supreme gift she gave me that night was to let me titty-ride those magnificent spheres of flesh, so firmly rounded with tight cleavage that made the perfect tunnel to contain my rampant dick.

I thrust between them until I came mightily, covering her lovely tits with my long spurts of hot jism until my juices dripped from her nipples. Before returning from leave to rejoin my unit in Belfast, needless to say I ordered a taxi every night, or rather the driver. She was an enthusiastic fuck as well. All in all she was a lady well worth getting up for.

C.S.M., Catterick

Only Make-Believe

Two sexy young guys are finishing repairing my television in the lounge when I look in on them. Straight from a shower, I'm wrapped in a towelling robe that shows my deep cleavage at the neck. They switch from station to station to make sure the TV is working, then choose a video from the pile beside the set. This should be interesting, I think wickedly, sitting on the settee and showing a good deal of white thigh. The video is a home movie.

The screen flickering into life shows me in the very room where we are now. I get excited by their presence as on screen I flounce about shedding my clothes in a good imitation of a seductive striptease. Both young guys are kneeling on the carpet, the way they were when repairing the set. They see that on the screen before them I'm down to a bra, suspender-belt and black stockings. As they turn to look at me in wonder, I smile. My cunt is already salivating – I imagine a tongue caressing the pouting lips. I loll back, the towelling robe falling open to give the boys a glimpse of my upper thighs and soft pubic mound.

So the video proceeds as they stay rooted to the carpet, watching my bra being discarded and big tits wobbling in close-up. My briefs are lowered with me facing away waggling the cheeks of my bottom at the camcorder before whirling around to show myself full frontal. I cup my tits as if offering them to a lover and let one hand sidle down over my belly to glide over my cunt-lips as I sway about to the background music.

On screen I shriek as my private strip is interrupted by two workman bursting in. They have seen me through the window as they arrive to empty the wheely-bin. I'm thrown down on the settee. There, held down, rolled over, my bottom smacked, I'm used as they like by the two burly intruders. Throwing off their work overalls, revealing hairy chests and huge erect pricks, I am made to suck on both their dicks, fucked back and front and am left slumped on the sofa as they leave. My hair, face and tits are smeared with their thick come. My legs, spread wide apart, show the pulsing and throbbing of my well-fucked pussy.

The viewing telly repair men turn to me and I smile at them. I say they can ask me any questions they like. I can see that massive erections tent the front of their jeans. I'm enjoying their amazed looks, letting the robe slip open to show more of my tits, even to the nipples, and a clear view of my hairy snatch. Of course I tell them I loved making the video, that I like sucking cocks, fucking and masturbating. When one asks if my husband had acted in the home porno shooting, I laugh and say he hadn't because I preferred taking different pricks. I could get his anytime.

'What does your husband think about that?' one asks. 'You taking other pricks up your quim and in your mouth, doesn't he object?'

'What if he does,' I say. 'Tough luck for him.'

'Aren't you afraid he'll ditch you? Get jealous and go away?'

'And leave this?' I ask, parting my legs even wider to show off my cunt while holding out my tits in my hands.

'Do you think he'd find another woman who'd take his cock in her mouth and swallow his jism? One who'd let him fuck her big tits as well as her pussy? He knows when he's on a good thing. Besides, he's big built. I wouldn't want him to leave. I love them big and thick.'

'Then how about this?' one of the lads says, drawing out his cock and advancing toward me. I take it in my mouth, its length and thickness filling my throat. 'Yes, suck it, you horny bitch,' he says, looking down at me suctioning on his big shaft. Much as I'd like it in my quim, I want to swallow all his sticky come. I want to hear him gasp in an agony of pure pleasure and have him buckle at the knees as I make him climax. As if defying me, he says, 'Suck all you want, my pretty one. I'll come when I'm ready.'

'And I'll fuck her at the same time,' I hear his mate say. He comes close and I see he has thrown off his shirt and jeans, a hugely rampant prick in his fist. For a moment I let the cock in my mouth slip out of my lips. 'That looks good,' I moan. 'Fuck me hard and deep. Fill me with your spunk. I don't care what you do as long as you fuck me with that lovely big prick. Fuck my cunt while your mate fucks my mouth . . .'

Rolled over unceremoniously, my arse is tilted up on the settee, with my chin resting on the arm at the other end. The plum-shaped head of a cock already well lubricated with my saliva is fed back into my mouth. At my upraised arse a long stalk of rigid flesh is guided between my bottom cheeks, aimed at the split lips of my rear-directed cunt. 'Yes, *yesss*!' I say with a mouth full of cock. As his whole length is thrust into me up to the balls, my fucker taunts me maliciously.

'Is your husband's dick as big and stiff as this?' he

says, ramming home all eight inches mercilessly, having me dipping my back to accept all there is. 'Does he fuck you as good as me?' With my mouth occupied I shake my head.

So it goes on, cocks thrusting into me from both ends. I come and come in multiple climaxes, my body jerking. I hear my two men groaning and know at last they are on the verge of coming. 'Ram it in my cunt and shoot it all up me,' I say as the cock I've been busy sucking is withdrawn from my mouth. I can guess what that means, even as I writhe in the ecstasy of the pounding of my quim, seeing the lad before me wanking himself in my face. Spurts of hot jism soaks my cunt as I open my mouth and a jet of spunk lands on my tongue. I try to swallow as fast as it arrives. Then his cock is back in my mouth to clean it for him.

It's a game we play, my hubby and I as we settle down in bed together. The object is to see who can tell the most erotic and arousing fantasy, one guaranteed to put us in the mood for a really furious fuck. I recommend it to all couples, especially if their sex sessions have become routine. My husband says I always come out with the best stories, claiming I'm more imaginative than he is. If he likes to think that, who am I to say otherwise?

Sarah, Portsmouth

Family Welcome

Anxious about what my mother would say, I kept my relationship with a black guy secret until I became pregnant. I then told her and so she met Troy. She said as long as he treated me and the baby right when it came, he was welcome in the family. Divorced from my dad, she said what her present husband thought did not matter. When we met Troy's father, a huge bouncer in a night club, my mum said he frightened her.

The wedding was at Troy's church and the reception at the night club where my new father-in-law was employed. My mum and I were the only white people therc, although our hosts could not have been kinder and made us feel at home. They had all clubbed together so that Troy and I could honeymoon on the Caribbean island where Troy's family came from. Mother was made a fuss of and given more drink than she was used to. Quite merry, she danced and had a great time, mostly in the company of Troy's dad, big Frank.

I lost contact with her during the evening, meeting all my new in-laws and later was told she had left for home. I wasn't worried about not seeing her leave as I'd be going home myself to change before heading for the airport and I'd say goodbye to her then. So, with Troy going to his house to change and meet me at Heathrow later, armed with wedding cake and a bottle of champagne I was driven home by Troy's sister, Lucy. When we arrived we saw no sign of my mum downstairs, nor was my stepfather home. That was no surprise as he always stayed in the pub until closing time. As for mum, I presumed she was next door with her neighbour, telling her about the wedding. Lucy came upstairs with me to help pack away my wedding dress.

Halfway up the stairs we were stopped by the sounds of people having sex. There were moans and grunts, the whimpering of a woman loving what was being done to her. Lucy and I exchanged glances, both having to cover our mouths to prevent our giggling. 'Your stepdad is doing his stuff,' Lucy whispered to me saucily. 'Your mum must have got home from the reception feeling like a bit.' I nodded my agreement, thinking it was about time, for I'd heard my mum moan that their sex life was once a month if she was lucky.

But I had a plane to catch and couldn't stay on the stairs, so Lucy and I tiptoed up to the landing still hearing the gasps and long-drawn-out sighs of a woman being pleasured. Going past the main bedroom, we found the door had been left half-open, allowing a full view inside. Facing us as he knelt at the foot of the bed, was the big black naked figure of Troy's dad. A pair of pale white legs were draped over his shoulders as Frank's head nuzzled between my mum's thighs. The joy he was giving her with his tongue in her cunt was obvious from her cries of delight.

I felt a trembling in my tummy as I couldn't help being excited by the erotic scene before me. I could imagine how moist and warm mother's cunt must have felt on his tongue, just juicily receptive for him to penetrate. That she would soon desire this was made clear when she began to beg him to fuck her. Shameful as it may seem, I wanted to watch and I stood rooted to the spot, unable to move. Lucy and I peered around the door. I wondered if she would draw me away, but a glance at her face showed she was mesmerised as her father stood up and fell forward between my mum's parted thighs.

From our viewpoint, Lucy and I saw Frank penetrate my mother with one deliberate lunge. His first thrusts were slow and deep. So responsive was my mum that we saw her bottom lifting from the bed as she matched his strokes, seeking every last inch of his huge black cock. Then, with all that hard flesh up her, my usually sensible parent began talking like a slut. Commanding him to do things to her in words I'd never have thought she'd utter.

In reply we heard big Frank assure her he'd 'Fuck her good. Fuck her crazy. You call me any time you want it, baby.' By her gasps and throaty pleas, it was obvious a climax was near. Her jerking and humping increased in pace. Then came a long drawn out '*Aaaarghh*' and spasms shook her body as Frank pistoned in and out of her, finally pumping his hot seed to the inner recess of mum's grasping quim. In the stillness that followed, Lucy plucked at my sleeve and we moved away, both shaken.

They were still on the bed and kissing and fondling, no doubt getting ready for a second bout, when Lucy and I tiptoed past their door and let ourselves out. Neither of us mentioned what we'd witnessed until well on the way to the airport, when Lucy who was driving began to giggle. 'That was some fuck,' she said at last, and I had to agree, joining her in such hearty laughter that she had to pull into a layby until we'd recovered.

'I only hope Troy is as good as his dad on our honeymoon,' I said.

'Have you heard the saying, there are no spare pricks at a wedding?' Lucy replied. Obviously my mum and

Troy's dad thought there shouldn't be.

I thought it was just a one-off, both of them letting their hair down after a boozy wedding reception. But it wasn't like that. One afternoon, after I'd returned from honeymoon, I popped over to visit mum. As I went in I saw a huge pair of men's shoes and a weatherproof anorak discarded at the foot of the stairs. Obviously mum was entertaining again or, rather, being entertained. I could hear sexually-inspired sounds coming from upstairs. I went into the kitchen to put the flowers I'd brought into a vase before turning to leave. On my way out my mother came downstairs, shocked to see me there. Her hair was mussed up, her eyes bright with that after-sex glow. It was obvious a dressing gown was all she wore.

I told her right away that what she did was her business and she had nothing to explain, leaving her with a kiss on the cheek. The next day she came to my place for coffee, rather shamefacedly admitting that Troy's father had been upstairs. She'd left him to go down to make him some tea when she bumped into me. Mum told me that for the first time in her life she was having satisfactory sex.

'I'm not giving Frank up, I love what he does to me,' she said excusing herself, and I remembered this was the mother I'd been scared to tell about my going out with a black guy! She and Frank evidently meet for a fuck every time the coast is clear which, by the way she looks nowadays, must be a hell of a lot.

Carole, Fulham

Loose Talk

My husband Freddie was doing very well at work, sent overseas on selling missions and trade fairs, his salary keeping us comfortably. Of course, the fact that his immediate boss Don was knocking me off on a regular basis did help considerably. Whenever Freddie was away, Don made it his business to see I didn't go without. By that I mean, he gave me sexual satisfaction in every position (and orifice) possible. I have to admit Don was a good lover who knew how to please a lady.

So I was having the best of both worlds, kept happy by Freddie when he was at home, and supplied by his boss Don whenever my husband was away. My mother used to say that your sins will find you out and so they did – in my case by a mere slip of the tongue.

One evening Freddie was due back from a trip to Germany, and greedy Don, who had had me all week, popped in during the afternoon to have me again. We were naked on the bed with Don idly kissing my bottom as I lay on my tummy, when he decided there was time for one more fuck before leaving.

His favourite method was to screw me face down and he was arousing himself (and me) by tonguing my slit from the rear. To aid him, I'd reached back to prise apart my cheeks to allow deeper access. Thus I was being nicely brought on by his tongue flicking over my outer lips, tickling the tight ring of my anus and titillating the erect nub of my clitty, all in the cause of making me beg f it. That was one of Don's quirks. Although hard as iron and eager to fuck, he would never do so until I asked for it.

'Please, fuck me, my darling. Fill me with your big cock now,' I'd say.

So his hard length would penetrate me, and I'd go on my elbows and knees, my back dipped and bum tilted to take every lovely inch of his thick stalk doggy-fashion. Even then he liked to taunt and humiliate me. 'What an arse you've got for screwing,' he'd say. 'Pity your husband can't satisfy you, Jean, it would save me having to do his job for him, keeping his randy slut of a wife satisfied.'

That afternoon I had no idea how many loads of spunk he pumped into me at both ends. So aroused could he get me that I was desperate to feel his big cock spurting into my mouth or cunny. From noon till after six he kept me naked on the marital bed, which was pushing his luck as I wasn't sure what time Freddie would return. I believe Don knew, but he enjoyed keeping me on edge. He had hardly dressed and gone when I heard the front door open and a loud hallo from downstairs told me my husband was back. And there was I still naked and recovering on the bed where Don had fucked me fore and aft for hours on end.

I answered back, saying I'd be right down, slipping on a cotton robe over my nakedness. It immediately clung to me because I was still damp with the sweat of my exertions. It was a warm spring evening and my nipples seemed stiffer and more prominent than I'd ever known, sticking out beneath the thin cloth of my robe. Going downstairs I saw Freddie standing beside his suitcase, eyeing me questioningly.

'What's up?' he asked. 'Why are you slinking around

half naked at this time of day?'

To gain time I put my arms around his neck and gave a tongue-probing kiss to welcome him home. 'My darling,' I said, a reasonable excuse coming inspirationally as I pressed my body to his. 'Forgive me, love, it's been such a lovely day that I've been working in the garden. I was about to have a bath when you arrived—' Still hugging him and even rubbing my crotch against the growing bulge in his pants, I added, 'Why not join me in the bath?'

Upstairs in our bedroom he looked at the unmade bed. 'I let things slide while you're away,' I said. 'I'd have made the bed later. It was too nice a day not to spend it gardening. I have to do these things with you away so much.'

'I miss things too,' Freddie said. 'You, for instance, looking like that with your nipples sticking up.' He put his hand between my thighs and whistled. 'And your quim feels wet. Naughty girl, you were playing with yourself when I arrived, weren't you?' He looked delighted, tickled pink to think of his wife pleasuring herself, something all men are curious about. He drew the robe from my shoulders and laid me across the bed. Thankful that I had got away with it, I opened my legs and offered myself gladly.

Kneeling before me, Freddie forced his tongue between the pouting lips of my cunt. He twiddled my already sensitive clitoris with the tip of his tongue, making me pull his head closer until it was enveloped in the warmth of my thighs. Expertly he tongued the length of my cleft, then thrust in as far as he could reach while I gave whimpering little cries of ecstasy, urging him on. With my body thrashing and writhing under the delicious ravishment, a shuddering climax building within my vitals, I squealed in dismay as Freddie's head lifted. *Don't stop, go on!* I urged him passionately.

'Shall I continue then?' he asked teasingly. 'Or would you rather have my prick? Say it, the tongue or a rigid bar of flesh up you?'

'Your prick, darling, your lovely big prick,' I answered at once, now desperate for it. 'Oooh, Freddie, fuck me now—'

My husband's erection was already poised and nuzzling my outer lips. Then he thrust forward and steered the circumcised knob deep into my well-drenched cunt. Iron hard, I gasped as the big rod stretched my innards and began to piston me to the brink. Soon the magnificent tool ramming my cunt set off jolting electric shocks in my lower belly and I was delirious, screeching for satisfaction.

'That's heaven,' I croaked, bucking and jerking out of control as the fucking continued. 'Harder, deeper, *Don*!' I heard myself shout. 'Fuck me harder, shove it all up! Oh, Don darling, don't stop – keep fucking me with your lovely big prick—'

Freddie's body suddenly ceased thrusting and then I realised the terrible and unforgivable *faux pas* I'd made. I had cried out *Don* in my excitement and used the name of my lover! Panic-stricken, I felt my husband's stiffness shrivel in my cunt, his manhood and pride deflated instantly by my slip of the tongue. Raising himself above me, there was hurt and anger in his eyes as he regarded me with scorn. 'You bitch!' he cursed me. 'You let that dirty sod fuck you, didn't you? Admit it, don't you dare lie to me.'

The one thing I didn't admit, that Freddie's promotion

at work had been through my giving Don his way with me, was something I did not reveal even during the heated argument that followed. I felt my husband had been hurt enough to add that to his shame of having an unfaithful wife. So he quit his job and we parted, something I shall always regret. He married again, as did I and our lives were completely changed through one moment's lapse. And my new husband? Don, of course, but I make sure he gets enough at home to stop him promoting staff for personal favours granted by their wives.

Jean, Middlesex

Blue Moves

It was another boring Wednesday. My wife was visiting her mother and after I'd taken her there in the car I went to the video library. It was quite empty, for rain was bucketing down and it was cold and dark outside. While browsing, my sense of smell was assailed by the powerful scent of a customer who'd come to stand beside me. A sideways glance showed she was a good-looking woman of about thirty; very shapely too, it seemed, for her raincoat could not disguise her curves.

I saw her looking around nervously and at last she spoke. 'Would you be a good friend?' she asked surprisingly. 'A man is following me and I came in here to get away from him. May I stand beside you as if we are together, in case he comes in?'

'Be my guest,' I said, not wanting to appear ungallant to a lady in need, especially such a good-looking one. She then asked me if I had a car outside. Hearing that I had, she suggested that if I drove her home she'd make it worth my while.

I couldn't believe she'd said it, but as we were standing close together she gave my tadger a friendly squeeze through my trousers. 'Please,' she repeated. 'I meant what I said. Wouldn't you like to fuck me, or have me suck you off? Perhaps both if you're greedy.'

'Are you for real?' I had to ask, the hand clasping my dong making it respond rigidly. That of course weakened any resolve I may have had. Leading her outside to my car, I found the street deserted, with not a sign of anyone loitering about to stalk the woman. Once inside the car, still not sure I was on a certainty, and not willing to start anything in case she screamed rape, I merely asked her where she lived and said I'd take her there. I remained hopeful, of course.

She directed me to a block of flats in a good area of town and then asked me in for a drink. Naturally I accepted the offer. The flat was spotless, well furnished, which confirmed my opinion that the woman was no scrubber. I asked for coffee as I was driving, so she went into the kitchen while I sat in her cosy lounge. When she reappeared carrying a tray, she was completely naked. Her body was beautiful: soft skin, big firm tits with erect nipples and a nicely rounded cunt with fuzzy hair smiling at me from the fork of her thighs.

I'd been pondering whether I should remind her about the fucking and sucking. Now that question was obviously redundant. The coffee was left on the coffee table as I stood up and threw off my clothes. Once I was bollock naked, she nodded in what I considered to be appreciation of my upright cock, took it in her hand and began to stroke it gently. Good as that was, I was delighted when she sank to her knees and closed her mouth over my rampant tool. At once she began to give me a superb blow-job as my knees buckled and I fucked her face, firing long spurts of spunk down her throat.

My bolt shot, temporarily at least, I was pushed back onto her long couch and mounted by her, with her legs straddling my face and broad well-spread arse inches above my nose. 'Now, lick,' I heard her say, and, looking up, all I could see was a moist cunt with parted outer lips descending over my mouth. At first she lightly rested her twat against my lips, so I began tracing my tongue around the entrance, gradually probing and flicking my tongue tip on the tight nub of her clitty.

Soon her pelvic movements began and she swivelled her quim against both my nose and chin as she helplessly climaxed. Collapsing beside me along the couch, she kissed me hard and long with open mouth and her tongue in deep, no doubt tasting her own juices on my lips. She was delightful to fondle, her skin butter soft and her breasts perfect to play with. Her hand was not idle, slowly and seductively stroking my prick back into life. As soon as she felt it was rigid enough she told me to fuck her – fuck her hard!

Again she took the initiative, straddling above me with her juicy cunt poised over my stander. I lay back and let her proceed, my gaze occupied with the sight of her two full breasts jiggling directly above my face. I felt her positioning my dick upright and nudging aside the swollen outer lips of her snatch before she eased it in an inch or two. 'Now do me!' she ordered sharply and bore down to impale herself to the hilt on my tool. To show her I was in full agreement, I lunged up with my hips and heard her cry out at the depth of my penetration.

Groaning, she urged me on, grinding down as I thrust up, my dick seemingly going deeper and deeper on each upward heave. Bouncing up and down with her cushiony buttocks slapping my thighs, her soaking cunt gripped my dick and sucked on it like a thirsty mouth. Holding back from injecting her with the hot spunk scalding my balls, I was relieved when she began to scream that she was coming, and she did so in long continuing spasms while I pumped my tribute into her. Sated and drained, I had not the strength to push her off me as she collapsed across my steaming body. It was easier to lay there under her weight, our skins tacky with sweat, savouring that fine after-sex feeling following a great session of screwing.

'Was anyone really following you?' I asked after we'd recovered and I'd resumed fondling her big tits, hopeful of another round before I had to collect my wife. 'I didn't see anyone around – not that I'm complaining about rescuing you.'

'Be at the video shop this time next week if you want to rescue me again,' she laughed. 'I'll be the most entertaining thing you could find in there.'

I didn't doubt it. So that we knew where we stood, I told her every Wednesday night I took my wife to her mother's and that I didn't mind a safe affair with no strings attached. She said she was married too, with a husband working overseas, and her desire was the same as mine – regular sex without complications. As I left her flat we had a long snog at her door and agreed to be friends in need. Taking my wife to her mother on a Wednesday is now the highlight of my week.

T.J., Gloucester

2. Get It While You Can

Bare Necessity
Fantasy Made Flesh
Personal Assistance
Father Knows Best
One Good Turn
Fancy a Ride?
Mouth to Mouth
In the Family
Fire Down Below
More Than One Way
Nice Little Earner

Bare Necessity

I'm a woman in my thirties, happily married with two lovely children. We have been married ten years and on average have sex at least twice a week. This is normally 'missionary position' coupling and I don't worry if I don't always come. Masturbation takes care of this.

Yes, I do pleasure myself, as I'm sure most women do, especially with a husband like mine who is not very adventurous in bed. For years I used my fingers but I sent away for a battery-operated vibrator when a friend showed me hers. One of my favourite fantasies is about this woman and how she seduced me – if that word applies since I was a willing victim and enjoyed every moment.

I've always liked women with large breasts and June certainly had big full tits. One day when I called at her house, she'd just got up and hadn't yet dressed. I went upstairs with her and sat down to chat while she took off her dressing gown and night dress before getting into the shower. As she stood before me nude I was unable to take my eyes off her superb breasts. She noticed this and teased me.

'Do you like them, Kath?' she asked, holding them up in her hands. 'Do they turn you on?'

My nipples and clitoris had become quite hard just looking at her naked body, and my vagina felt itchy with the moistness down there. I said I was amazed at how big and shapely they were and that was why I was staring.

'Don't you have even a tiny bit of lesbian desire in you?' she asked, standing over me so that her breasts loomed over my face. 'I do and I'm not ashamed of it, it can be such a relief after my husband's idea of lovemaking. Is your man any good in bed?'

I admitted that Charles was not. June then lay down on her back on the bed. It was the first time I'd seen a woman stroke her own vulva, trailing her fingers up and down the prominent lips. 'Why don't you undress and let me look at you?' she said calmly. Although I was trembling with nerves I took off my clothes. She remarked how much bushier and darker my pubic hair was than hers and said that I had a nice 'pouty' pussy. The way she was talking made me feel sexy. Soon I was very aroused.

She took my wrist and pulled me down on the bed beside her, her hands touching my breasts and between my legs. I let her carry on and responded to the long passionate kiss she gave me with tongue extended, my first with another woman. I didn't care, only wanting to be brought to climax by her. I whispered between kisses that I wished she would make me come. She replied that if I really wanted it she would finish me off. It was all very erotic with our breasts and nipples touching, our bare skin pressing together as we embraced.

June then licked and sucked my breasts before slipping down between my legs to perform cunnilingus on me, something my husband didn't like and I'd given up asking for. It was a tremendous thrill and I lay back and let her bring me off by sucking my clitoris. Then I fondled her big breasts and suckled on them as she fingered me, which was enough to make me come twice more. Later we went shopping and parted with a lingering kiss and an unspoken agreement that we'd have more sessions. I made dinner for my husband and children that night with an inner glow as I remembered my unusual day.

I didn't consider myself an unfaithful wife. Being with another woman didn't make it like adultery. In my next session with June she took her vibrators from her bedside cabinet and introduced me to the delights of a strap-on dildo, mounting me like a man and successfully bringing me to orgasm until I was drained. The next time we went shopping in the city, June and I dined in a hotel restaurant with two presentable men who had chatted us up at the bar. I knew June was keen to take things further and was caught up in the excitement of an illicit dalliance myself. The four of us spent the afternoon in one of the rooms they had rented.

It was another first. June and I were naked together on the double bed with the men equally nude, taking us in turn. I was licked, sucked, fingered and fucked in varying positions all afternoon. It was my first time of having sex with another man let alone two of them. It has never been repeated but is an experience I savour, the sort of thing I think all women should try. When the men were temporarily exhausted, June and I gave them a lesbian show that soon had them sitting up and watching avidly. Sometimes I wonder if Charles would appreciate seeing me making love to another woman.

Perhaps he would, but I've never dared suggest it. June broke up with her husband and moved away and is now living in London with a woman lover. This is an account of my extra-marital flings and I don't think this makes me a sex maniac, a slut or bad wife. I would not change my life except to have my husband become more sexually aware. Ordinary wives *do* step out of line at times – it's almost a necessity.

Kathleen, Berkshire

Fantasy Made Flesh

So-called sex experts claim to reveal women's secret fantasies. This always makes good reading, especially for guys like me. It's a turn-on to think your old school-teacher Miss Prim probably fancied being bound to her bed by her wrists and ankles while being ravaged. Or fantasised about being gang-banged by a group of labourers with ten-inch cocks.

I've no doubt that everyone has their own kinky fantasies. Mostly they remain just wishful thinking. What I'm describing here is what happened when a woman tried to get me to live out her fantasy without me being aware of the fact. I was a fresh-faced twenty at the time and I suppose looked even younger. Fresh out of art college, I was employed by a firm of graphic designers. My boss was a young married woman in her early thirties.

Concepta was attractive in a wholesome way, with an average figure. I found her friendly, felt 'in' with her because she gave me my quota of the most interesting work. She talked about her husband a great deal and was over the moon about being married. One night, to celebrate the completion of a successful display for a prestige business, us members of the art department dined out in town. Connie, as she was known, although I always addressed her as Mrs C, insisted I share her taxi after-wards. She paid off the taxi outside her house, although I still had a bus ride to my tiny flat. Slipping her arm through mine, she walked me to her front door.

In the darkness of a large porch, she thanked me for seeing her safely home and kissed me on the mouth. I was shocked as much as surprised, more so when she pulled my arms around her and kissed me again, this time quite lingeringly. 'You're so wicked, Simon,' she said. 'Wanting to kiss me like that with my husband just on the other side of this door.' Still in shock, I was kissed again and, with her comfortable cushiony body pressed to mine, I responded to the kiss and tried to slide my tongue into her mouth.

'Please, don't, Simon,' she said as if it were me who was forcing the pace. My dick had got mightily stiff and was nestling snugly against the plump bulge of her quim. I even managed to get in a couple of jiggles against it before she held me off. Then she became serious, putting her hand over my mouth as if to stop me kissing her again.

'I know you are young, and young people are so eager that I can forgive you for trying,' she said, 'but you must realise I'm a happily married woman as well as your superior at work. I trust this silly attempt of yours to make love to me will remain our secret. No one must ever know. I'm sure you'll respect a married woman's wish—'

'There she goes about being married again,' I said to myself as I went off with a boner so stiff I almost limped. Of course I'd found snogging her fun, but no thought of chatting her up or pulling her had previously entered my head. How could it? She was my boss, at least twelve years older, and married. There was that married thing again. It was as if that was the thrill of it, the kick, being just a little naughty in a way that a nice married woman shouldn't behave.

Why me? I wondered. I supposed I was handy, also not liable to boast about our shared kisses in the office. I thought it a one-off after a celebratory night out. On subsequent occasions however, still frequently reminding me she was a married woman, she enticed me to kiss her in the privacy of her office. She was nice, mind you, good to cuddle and kiss and have the odd feel of her tits through her blouse, but she only allowed mild petting so I packed her in and concentrated on a girl who was a definite fuck. This annoyed Connie and I started getting the dull jobs in the office and being sharply spoken to about my work.

She had a key to my flat and I often found her in my room when I returned after an evening out. It seemed her husband was never suspicious. As a senior executive at the firm, she probably told him she was working late and he accepted that. I wondered if her strict religious upbringing had anything to do with her obsession to be unfaithful or whatever. Anyway, she came to my flat and so I always tried to seduce her. Without success, I may add, trying harder each time until our sessions became wrestling matches! Of course I didn't push it to the limit and she'd straighten her clothes and leave me bone-hard.

Yet she'd always return for more, sometimes waiting in my room until I returned very late after sex with my girlfriend. One night I came back after drinking with some mates and she was sitting on my single bed as usual. It struck me she *wanted* me to be rough with her. This could have led to trouble but after long kisses and squeezes at her firm tits, I took the chance. For over an hour we struggled and sweated, grunted and groaned. I'd managed to pull off her dress but was ready to quit.

Her defence was really strenuous but she made no

attempt to get away. I never would have stopped her from leaving the room. At last I sat up on the bed beside her, giving up. Again she made no attempt to retrieve her dress and leave, looking at me expectantly. So I took a breather and began again until I had her below me on the bed in a completely revealed state. I knew, despite her struggles and protests, that she'd helped me get her naked. Now her bra was off and breasts out, the nipples suspiciously erect. Her briefs had been dragged over her ankles and, with her legs spread, I saw her plump split quim with its mass of thick hair.

But I was exhausted and gasping for air. In the wrestling I'd lost my erection. 'Don't stop, fuck me,' I heard her whisper from below. Encouraged, I got my boner back by kissing her breasts and sucking her nipples. While doing this I held her spreadeagled arms down by the wrists which I'm sure she liked, judging by the protests that started anew. Then I went down between her thighs and sucked her labia into my mouth and tongued her while she groaned and made whimpering noises. You want it, you bitch, I thought, and penetrated her to the hilt with my prick sliding up a very lubricated cunt.

Almost immediately she began to convulse under me, beginning to thrust her cunt up to my lunges as I buried my knob to the last inch in her churning quim. Even as she went into spasms and climaxed strongly, she was pleading 'No, no, please no! Don't you know I'm a married woman, you dirty beast?' Despite these entreaties, she humped with her bottom pounding the bed and her legs locked around me. She held me so tight that, as my surge of sperm threatened to drench her love-tunnel, I feared putting a baby into her.

She may have wanted to be fucked but I'm sure getting preggy didn't figure in her plan. As she twisted and writhed, I withdrew and heaved my body up, shooting my surprisingly copious load of creamy spunk over her tits and up to her chin. She then rolled aside and began calling me names, abusing me for 'forcing and taking' her like that. I knew she was secretly relieved and pleased I had not spunked inside her. Asking for a handkerchief, she began to dab at the come splattering her tits.

'You really are a dirty beast, Simon,' she went on, but made no attempt to dress or even cover her nudity. I could only surmise she wanted a fling, an outside fuck, without appearing casually unfaithful to her husband. I had 'forced' her so her conscience was clear. She even insisted on repeats, coming to my room and lolling on my bed in open invitation. In the end I took another post in another town to escape her. Fucking Connie was too much like hard work.

Simon, Wimbledon

Personal Assistance

When I divorced my Steve to marry Clifford, it was to take up the offer of the good life, to escape drudgery and financial worries. Steve and I had been together over two years, during which time I'd been the breadwinner. The only thing we had in common was lusty sex. We may have argued and fought during the day but each night we fucked like it was going out of fashion. I needed my nookie.

An experienced secretary, by the age of twenty-three I had worked my way up to become the big boss's personal assistant, although I know my appearance and thirty-eight-inch bosom had been helpful. From the first moments in Clifford's private office, he gave notice that my duties included letting him fondle my boobs and touch up my bottom. I didn't object; I hoped it would lead to rewards. I envied his lifestyle: the Rolls, expensive suits, Caribbean holiday villa and a mansion-sized home in Surrey.

He was divorced from his third wife, so was free and back on the market. My marriage to Steve notwithstanding, within a week my boss had me across his desk, fucking me. 'Despite that curvy figure, those superb tits and arse, and the fact I've been mentally undressing you all week,' he said bluntly, 'you're still expected to operate efficiently as my personal assistant.' I couldn't think of any great foul-ups I'd made, but let's face it, I had a top salary and a job that promised foreign travel, so I acted contrite, hanging my head as if in fear.

He obviously liked that. Perched on the edge of his huge desk, slapping his palm with a ruler, he questioned me about how I should be punished for being careless in my work. I instinctively knew he was a spanker, one who got his kicks paddling a bare female bum. He ordered me to strip, and I guessed a preliminary to a fucking would be a few warming smacks on my botty – nothing too painful, I hoped. Intrigued by the thought of a big girl like myself being thrashed, I felt undeniable arousal. I'd read about spanking for fun being a turn-on and that a well-paddled tush sent a quim a-throbbing and I was eager to find out for myself.

'Strip,' he ordered me sharply once again, so I stood before him and disrobed. His authority and power of command had me weak at the knees. Being utterly under his control was a relief – I didn't have to care, I could just go with the flow. No doubt I felt thus through continually having the worries of running a home and paying a huge mortgage with a layabout husband who would neither work nor lift a finger to help. I found being dominated a whole new experience and accepted gratefully that I was being made to obey.

It was both thrilling and humiliating, but I could not resist undressing before Clifford. The way his eyes devoured my tits and belly made me shiver. He stood aside, indicating the top of the desk and I obediently leaned over the tooled leather surface until my breasts were flattened and my bare bottom was properly tilted for his enjoyment. 'A fine arse,' I heard him murmur, then felt a hand gently gliding over both smoothly rounded cheeks as if savouring the feel of my flesh. I remained bent over for his pleasure, hardly a dignified position for a naked female to be.

But it was exciting too, and I felt even more vulnerable as his palms separated my full cheeks, prising them apart. I cringed, thinking of what he could see in the crevasse revealed: the split rearward-pointing mound of my cunt with its tangle of pubic hair, and just above that the tightly puckered ring of my arsehole. I heard him draw in his breath then felt a curled finger enter my quim. Once beyond the moistened lips, I almost sucked his other fingers inside. It was too much. I squirmed my bottom to the fingering, worked it back against his hand. 'Bring me off, make me come with your fingers or your tongue, I don't care!' It was my voice begging him, and not for any reason but my own demanding need.

His fingers were withdrawn, then his face pressed into my nether cheeks, his tongue entering me and circling around my highly responsive clitoris. 'Yes, tongue-fuck me,' I heard myself cry. 'Bring me off!'

In reply I was told sharply that *he* was in command, not I. 'You crafty bitch,' he added. 'Hoping to escape your punishment by trying to seduce me, were you? You'll pay extra for that.' The sting of the ruler brought down sharply on my rear made me cry out. He gave me a good dozen strokes to warm my bottom before he stopped.

Turning to see what would be his next move, I saw him unzip his trousers and reveal a grossly swollen prick. Leering at me, he held his stiffened stalk at the base, stroking it gently. Then he directed the bulbous knob between my cheeks, rubbing it against my outer lips, making them gape for his entry. I was desperate for full penetration. 'Fuck me, fuck me, fuck me!' I gasped.

'I can see I'm going to have to be very firm with you,' he said. 'Teach you who exactly is the boss.' Despite that, he drove into me, punching his whole length up my pulsating cunt.

His thrusts were slow and excrutiatingly sensuous, making me gurgle with the lewd pleasure of being stuffed with rigid flesh. I squeezed my thighs and could feel his massive erection sandwiched between the muscled walls of my interior. Though gripped, his stalk pistoned easily in the lubricated tunnel. He ordered me to talk dirty and say how it felt with his cock up me and how good he was. He demanded to know if my husband was as big as he was. Revelling in his power over me, he rode me faster and harder, ordering that I tell him when I was coming. He need not have worried, my agitated thrusting as my rear buffeted his belly told him all he needed to know as I had a shattering climax.

These and many other variations became routine in my time in his office. The cane, the strap and the ruler were resorted to when I was supposedly disobedient or careless. At times I was ordered to crawl under his desk and, after kissing his penis into erection, take his stiffened cock into my hungry mouth and suck him dry.

In time, after my divorce from Steve, I became Clifford's fourth wife. I was under no illusion that he dished out his kind of discipline to my replacement, a pretty twenty-year-old, or that he fucked her regularly. To make up for that, I visited Steve whenever I felt like a change of dick. I'm also friends with two of Cliffords ex-wives, both of them living in luxury from large separation payments, so if the worst comes to the worst and he exchanges me, I'll make sure he pays up. One thing he isn't, is mean. I don't think he'll leave me, however. His other wives were jealous of his other women. I'm never possessive or demand to know where he's been or with whom. He can bring his latest lovers home if he wants to. Could be fun making up a threesome. I'd enjoy tanning their pretty arses myself.

Sondra, London

Father Knows Best

My three sisters all had babies. They laughingly claimed, when teasing me about being childless, that their husbands only had to hang their trousers up at the end of the bed to make them pregnant. My husband Rob, I was certain, had a low sperm count or was infertile. It seemed that no matter how broody I got or how much we fucked, I was not to get the little one I longed for. So I make no apology for my deception and tell it here as a matter of interest to women desperate for a baby. Where there's a will, there's always a way.

Of course, now broody females can get fertility treatment and have babies in their later stages of life. There was nothing like that for me and, as the years went by, it seemed I would never get my wish to be a mother. I envied women with huge pregnant bellies and those pushing prams. So I decided to do something about it.

Everyone knows a standing cock has no conscience and that a horny man, given encouragement by a girl he fancies, will not turn down the chance to fuck her. I knew this was true even as my husband's dad worked his rampant dick up my aching cunt. The eagerness with which he rammed in every inch until his balls slapped against my cushiony bum, the way he grunted out how he had always longed to fuck me, answered any doubts I may have had about seducing my father-in-law. He wanted to fuck me as much as I wanted him to flood me with his hot sperm and get me in the club. Although I had to admit, as I gripped my legs around his back and humped against him, he was a great shag.

That first time was a balmy spring day. Dad, as I called him, drove a long-distance truck, going regularly to Europe. Whenever in our area he always looked in, his home being in Lancashire. On that day I welcomed him and invited him to lunch, serving the meal in the thin summer frock, well aware it showed off my twin cheeky buttock moons and shapely legs. I knew he'd told Rob that I was a fine well-built girl and guessed he fancied me. Looking at him, I thought how handsome and strong he was, the ideal man to make a kid.

As I served him his food at the table, I allowed one soft pliant breast to press into his shoulder. My quim began to pulse and twitch and I knew that I wanted him. Wanted him to fuck me, have me naked in bed, giving me every rigid inch of his prick. Unable to resist, I sat down on his lap, slipping his arm around my waist and directing his hand to cup my right tit. The nipple thickened as he stroked it through my dress. Our faces turned to each other and we shared a long open-mouthed kiss, our tongues probing as we clung together.

In my haste to let him see and fondle my naked breasts, I lost patience trying to unbutton the neck of my dress and tore it open to the waist. Realising my urgency and with the same desire, my father-in-law's hands reached behind me to unhook my bra and release my boobs. I nursed his head and held each teat in turn to his lips, while he sucked like he was a hungry baby. My contented sighs and moans were evidence of my excitement. Seated as I was on his lap, I squirmed my bottom against the rigid cylinder of flesh fitted snugly into the crease of my cheeks. As I worked against it, he began thrusting motions to meet my movements.

For the first time in our torrid embrace, I spoke between kisses. 'I want you to fuck me,' I pleaded. He agreed readily. His left hand was already under my dress, my briefs sodden at the crotch as he stroked my split lips through the thin cotton. Under my bottom his prick seemed of unbending hardness, making me weak at the thought of taking it up my cunt. 'The bedroom,' I urged him. 'Take me there. Fuck me in comfort.'

We were pulling off our clothes even as I shamelessly led him into the room where I slept with my husband. Stretched out before him on the bed, I raised my bottom to allow him to pull off my knickers, leaving me naked. His fingers found my pouting cunt lips then my clitoris. My quim was really juiced up, squelching as he fingered me, making me think hopefully that it would be receptive to making me pregnant.

He was no amateur at arousing a woman and could have given his son pointers. Hushed tones were used as he admired my body, all the while kissing and sucking my nipples as I arched my back and pushed my tits into his face. Almost delirious with lust, I begged him to fuck me. His tongue delved into my belly button and then my hands directed his head downwards, tilting my pubic mound until his nose and mouth were buried in the tangle of cunt hair. His tongue slipped between my outer lips, probing deep within me.

'Eat me, suck me, I love it, you horny sod,' I ground out between clenched teeth, gyrating my hips in ecstasy as he captured my clit in his lips and sucked on the tight bud greedily. Then I remembered the object of the exercise: much as I was loving the tonguing, it was all about getting me in the family way. 'Don't make me come like that,' I told him. 'I want your big prick up me. Please, stick it into me, shoot your load up me while I'm coming! Fuck me hard and long—'

But even while getting across me as I widened my thighs to be mounted, he hesitated. 'I've never wanted to fuck anyone as much,' he said, '*but what if I make you pregnant?*' With the plum-sized knob of his big stander nudging the pouting lips of my eager twat, my answer was inspired. 'You won't do that,' I said impatiently. 'Your son has already seen to that and put me in the club. Fuck me all you want, let it all go.' At once I felt his forward lunge and cried out in delight as his shaft slid up me to the balls.

It had never felt so good and, of course, doing something wrong and wicked (like seducing your father-in-law to give you a baby!) is guaranteed to add to the arousal. I screamed for him to give me every inch he had, pleading and moaning that I wanted more. His mouth seemed fused to mine as he rode me, squeezing my tits fiercely in his excitement. In response, I clutched him with my arms and legs, tilted my arse, bucked to his thrusts until our sweat-soaked bellies slapped like handclaps. When he fired his volley of hot jism into me, I almost passed out as I climaxed with him, my innards drenched.

Even as he rolled aside I held him, thanking him for a wonderful fuck, kissing him passionately and begging him not to leave. 'You are some girl,' he said, toying with my tits, 'although I'm as bad, fucking my son's wife. I've always wanted to, but that's no excuse. What was yours? Isn't my lad giving you enough?' I admitted we were naughty doing what we did, but I fancied him too. His son would never know, so what harm was there in trying each other? 'It's a good job you're pregnant,' he said. 'I'm sure I'd have put a baby into you.' To make sure he had, after some more fondling, kissing and cuddling, I sucked his cock until it grew spectacularly.

Of course the obvious thing was to use it on me again, this time with me mounting him. Sharing a bath made us both very randy again, and now it was with me on my elbows and knees, his prick wet with my saliva sliding in deep to my furthest recess. Encouraging him, my bottom jerking as he fucked me, to ensure I stood every chance of conceiving I once again was soaked by his spurts of hot come.

Sure enough, a few weeks later I felt the definite signs of pregnancy: upset tummy with morning sickness, cravings for certain foods (pickled onions in my case), tender and swollen breasts with sore nipples. My husband's father had fathered a child in me.

Rob does not know until this day. They do say it's a wise child that knows its own father. My husband was delighted to think he had 'put one in me' as he liked to crow. In later months when I was as stretched as a belly could get and my breasts were huge, he'd swagger about feeling no end of a man. On the other hand, Rob's dad had no idea he was the real father. When our boy was born, a real healthy specimen, my hubby was quite touched when I suggested we name the new arrival Gordon, after his dad. I thought that only fair!

Isobel, Dumfries

One Good Turn

As a teenager, I was invited to go with my best friend Kev and his parents on their Spanish seaside holiday. I jumped at the chance because my own parents were no fun to go with and my little sister was a pain. The main reason though was because Kev's mum was a real honey, a fluffy blonde with a curvaceous hourglass figure. I was well aware of this because that summer I'd seen her sunbathing in the garden. She wore a miniscule bikini which she filled, or rather overflowed, like a contestant in Miss World.

The thought of ogling her for a whole ten days on the beach was the stuff of wet dreams for a randy youth like me. I had already enjoyed long sneaky looks at her big tits and the way they jiggled under a tight sweater. And, although she was approaching forty, I suppose, the figure-hugging mini-skirts she wore clung to her lovely firm bum, moulding the well-rounded cheeks atop her long shapely legs.

From the first day, May went topless at the beach and hotel pool. I was able to ogle her bountiful boobs and thick pink nipples quite unrestricted. Her excuse for bikini briefs didn't hide much – a triangular patch of nylon covering the plump mound of her twat, held in place by a G-string which dived between her arse cheeks. I heard her husband complain she showed too much, and her son was embarrassed. But there were no complaints from me or any of the other males of all ages who eyed her charms appreciatively.

Kev and his dad were sports maniacs. They spent hours water-skiing, para-gliding and snorkelling – which left me alone with May and that was no chore. However, she'd got chummy with the waiter who served our table, a youth not many years my senior with olive skin and black eyes, built like an athlete. He joined us at the beach or pool when off duty, which made me feel like telling him to fuck off or I'd tell her husband he was bothering her. I couldn't do that, of course, so I smouldered, mad as hell from jealousy. The bastard wore a black swimming pouch bulging like he had a prick of abnormal size and I knew May was well aware of it.

One morning, with Kev and his dad out fishing at sea for the day, I changed into my swimming trunks after breakfast and went to the pool. There I awaited the gorgeous May, or rather her luscious tits, and was disappointed when she didn't turn up. When there was no sign of her I went up to her room. My hand was raised to knock on the door when I paused, a second sense telling me to leave it. I noticed the door was open a mere inch or so. Touching it gently with a fingertip, I silently opened it as much again. Then the low groan of pleasure and muttered words I heard coming from inside the room stopped me in my tracks.

It was unmistakably the sound of a woman being pleasured, and the ecstatic murmuring continued as I dared to look around the door. May and the young waiter stood beside the bed, their clothes strewn at their feet. Her breasts looked so firm and ripe, no doubt swollen with arousal and the lucky Spanish waiter was nuzzling them, sucking on each nipple as she tilted her teats up for his kisses. 'Now fuck me,' I heard her sigh. 'Fuck me hard, shove that big prick right up me.'

'You dirty bitch,' I swore silently between clenched teeth. It was burning envy. I wished it were me.

He lowered her to the bed on her back and positioned himself to fuck her. As he turned, my eyes feasted on his cock for the first time, in awe at its size and thickness as it reared before him. I saw May's eyes gleam as she savoured the thought of taking all that rigid flesh up her. In anticipation, she spread her thighs and I could see her puffy cunt lips open and wet with her juice. 'Fuck me, Juan,' I heard the greedy cow tell him again – he was obviously experienced at giving women the full treatment. He leaned forward and began to press long kisses around her cunt. Whimpering her pleasure, May raised her knees and pulled his face into her crotch.

I could picture his nose nestling in her forest of fair pubic hair, and his tongue lapping inside her love-hole as she squealed and bucked her arse from the bed in her ecstasy. She cried out loud that he was making her *come*, then that she was *coming*! While she writhed in the after affects of her climax, he held her upper thighs apart with his palms and prepared to spear her. His prick was by far the biggest I had ever seen, but every inch of it went in as she guided it between her cunt lips. Watching was agony. My prick tented out my swimming trunks as hard as steel.

Juan played her like a fish, at times thrusting hard and making her buck to him wildly. Then he'd shaft her slowly, drawing out his big cock to the knob and pausing while she screamed for him to shove it back in, demonstrating to me just how unladylike females can get when made lewd and desperate for the dick. Juan's expertise was also a lesson on how to fuck a woman to distraction.

Much as I resented him making free with May, I had to admire his skill, no doubt honed by fucking all the neglected married Englishwomen who stayed at his hotel. I saw him bring May off time after time until he rolled aside from her, leaving her spreadeagled on her back, with her legs widespread and cunt steaming. Looking up, she saw me at the door.

Juan saw me too and sat up in alarm. I heard him say to May that I'd tell her husband, but before I could say that I wouldn't she smiled at me and got off the bed, her tits swaying enticingly. She came over and, without a word, pulled down my trunks, allowing my cock to spring up level with my belly. She took it gently in her hand and led me back to the bed. 'Fuck me,' I heard her say once more, only this time to me! She guided my hand between her legs and I felt how wet she had become. 'Fuck me, Peter. Fuck my cunt from behind,' she said, turning on her hands and knees on the bed.

So she knelt on the bed facing the dressing-table, urging me to mount her doggy-style. I could see myself in the mirror. While I was hesitating, eager but still overawed, she teased me. 'Come on,' she giggled. 'I've seen you ogling my titties all week. Ever since you've come home with Kev I've known you wanted to fuck me.' This was true enough. I'd been chums with her son since I was fourteen, and I'd had fantasies about shagging my mate's mum since then. Reaching between her legs, she took hold of my rampant dong and inserted it between her cunt lips.

She tilted her arse even more to give me better access, so I gripped her hips and pressed home my knob between the upraised cheeks of her cushiony backside. Not to be left out, Juan knelt up before her and fed his slack prick to her lips. She gobbled it into her mouth, sucking avidly as I shagged her at the other end. My prick shunted in her like a hot knife in butter, even with her using the muscles of her cunt-walls to squeeze my stalk. 'Fill my cunt with spunk, Pete!' she ordered, her lips parted before Juan's dick and about to resume sucking him. 'Juan can come in my mouth too!' It was too much to expect me to hold out, so I thrust into her mightily and sent spurt after spurt of my juice deep into her innards.

While May's husband and her son continued to pursue their healthy outdoor activities, May, Juan and I were glad to follow our own programme of lustful indoor activities. The lady was used to the full, with her complete agreement. I spent the following week in a kind of daze, shagging as much as I could manage. May thrived on having two young men to service her and she became quite cheeky with it. Once at breakfast, before her hubby left for water-skiing lessons, she teased him that she was being sexually neglected while he tired himself out each day and was no use to her at night.

'I'll have to find an obliging waiter who'll help me out,' she laughed brazenly. 'Like Juan, for instance. Do you think he'd find an older woman like me suitable as a holiday lover?' I didn't know where to look, but May's husband seemed to find it funny. 'Don't kid yourself,' he chortled. 'A good-looking young bloke like that can have his pick.' Which only shows what he knew! However, I'm sad to say that, once back home, May put up the shutters. It was just a holiday fling – for which I shall always be grateful.

P.R.L., Derbyshire

Fancy a Ride?

Being widowed in the prime of my life meant missing out on the regular sex my late husband and I enjoyed so lustily. Suddenly friends began to stop asking me to their parties. I knew, as a well-upholstered woman of fifty who could be taken for thirty-five, that wives found me a danger. I was a good-looking widow on the loose whom their husbands made a fuss of. This spell of celibacy, doing without except what I could do to myself, taught me I needed sex more than ever.

Then I found myself driving a neighbour's son back to college for the new term. Brian was twenty, very handsome and hard-bodied, with a smile that made teenage girls swoon. I'd seen the way they flocked around him at barbecues by the pool in his parents' large garden. Until I became an available woman again, I'd been a regular guest with my husband at these garden parties and swimming afternoons. Now that too had stopped. However, with my neighbour's two cars unavailable, (the husband had one away on business and the other was being fixed after a bash in a car park) I was considered safe enough to drive the boy back to university.

Seeing Brian looking bronzed and fit after his vacation, at once reminded me of how lonely and horny I was. Although it didn't occur to me he would look at me as anything more than a friend of his mother's. We had not been driving long when he grinned at me, saying, 'You know, I could have gone back by train and saved you this trip but I wanted the chance to be alone with you, Ellen.' He dropped his hand on my leg above my knee and gave it a lingering I-like-the-feel-of-that squeeze. The way he returned my enquiring look was hopeful. I'd seen it in other men.

'Why the sudden urge to be with me then, young man?' I asked, doing nothing to knock his hand away from my leg. Rain was pelting down outside and I wasn't going to engage in what promised to be an interesting conversation while driving along a country road. I drew into a lay-by and pulled up, turning in my seat to face him. 'What's the big attraction?'

'You,' he said, his hand moving up my thigh, higher and higher, inching up under my skirt. 'My mother doesn't want you around when my father is at home. She knows he fancies you. I don't blame him. I think you are the sexiest woman I've ever seen—'

'You shouldn't say such things,' I heard myself muttering. I'd been so long in the sexual wilderness that I could not resist the young man even though I was as old as his mother. I opened my legs so that his wandering hand was now at the gusset of my brief panties, two fingers stroking through the thin material directly on the pursed lips of my sex. I felt a rush of emotion. The groping fingers had me soaking my briefs, my pubic mound beginning to thrust back against his fingering.

Enough was enough, I turned off the engine, grabbed him in my arms and kissed him, crushing my mouth to his. It became a long and lewd snog, with intense passion both sides. Our tongues entwined, invading our mouths. I felt Brian's free hand on my right breast, cupping and squeezing. '*Yesss*,' I moaned in ecstasy and begged him to play with my tits, to suck on my nipples, to feel my pussy, my bottom, *everything*. 'Oh, I will, I've always wanted to since I was a boy. I've dreamed of having you.'

This to a sex-starved widow was the stuff of wild fantasies, where virile toyboys fucked older women to exhaustion and multiple climaxes. He fumbled as he opened my blouse and I helped him. 'I want you naked,' he hissed, demanding in his own urgency. 'Let's move into the rear, it's roomier along the back seat.'

It was madness, I knew, but as eager as he I got out in the teeming rain and climbed in the rear. Throwing off our clothes in the cramped space as the windows steamed up, we were both soon completely nude. I saw his firm young muscled body and rigidly erect penis and my insides melted. I lay back along the seat, one leg over the edge and, showing off my bush of hair, offered him my cunt.

He was entranced with my body. Bending over, he sucked on each nipple in turn while I held up my breasts for him, cupped in my hands like a nursing mother. This while his curled finger sought and entered my sopping cleft, making me work my bottom against the seat. With his lips around a nipple, he muttered that none of his college girlfriends were stacked like me and that he adored my mature curves and full breasts. As he fingered me I felt pure pleasure coursing through my cunt, throbbing and clenching. So help me, I heard myself begging him to put his prick right up me.

Positioned as he was, above me and between my legs, it was I who guided his cock to my pussy lips, sighing my delight as he slid inch after long inch of hard youthful dick into my eagerly awaiting cranny. My legs locked around his back, my hands cupping and pulling on his firm buttocks to draw him closer. Driving into me to the balls, he had me screaming out for him to give me all he had and my writhing and jerking bottom was pounding the car seat as I came. Outside the car a fierce thunderstorm raged, rain drumming on the car roof as Brian too reached his climax, his rod working into my quim like a piston as long jets of his hot sperm drenched me.

Undisturbed, we cuddled up naked, fondling and kissing until a second longer-lasting fuck occurred. This time we switched places, Brian under me as I rode his prick. Resting after this bout, he told me that he'd fantasied over me as a schoolboy, struck by my figure in a bikini when I'd swum in his parents' pool. During term we exchanged letters saying in the plainest terms what we would do to each other during his vacations. Much in the same lewd tone was said in the phone calls he made.

It was my first, but by no means my last, sexual experience with that young man. Brian, for all his youth, really knows how to satisfy a lady. What he lacks in experience, he makes up for in enthusiasm – besides he's a quick learner. When he comes home on holidays, we have plenty of chances to meet in secret and we make the most of them all. I'll always be there for him, and when he goes to parties with girls his own age, it's me he sneaks in to take to bed. His mother keeps me out of the way in case I make a play for her husband, but why should I do that when I have her son!

S., Wiltshire

Mouth to Mouth

This is a joint letter composed with my dear wife who, after over thirty years of marriage, still agrees with me that oral sex between us is as arousing and erotic as ever. My initiation into going down on a female was over forty years ago when, believe me, licking a woman out, putting one's mouth to a cunt, was considered very perverted. My first attempt at tongue-fucking was not with a teenage girl of my own age (I was seventeen) but with a middle-aged married woman, the same age as my mother and a close friend of hers.

Come to think of it, if I'd suggested licking out any of the gymslipped virgins I tried to kiss and feel without success, they'd have been disgusted and called me a dirty beast. At least that's what I like to think, but who knows what lurid fantasies those prim misses had when fingering their tight little cunnies?

Elizabeth, the lady who first got me to 'eat beaver', succeeded in seducing me in her bedroom and gave me a love for the taste of cunt which remains to this day.

I'd gone to her house at my mum's suggestion to help Elizabeth put back up high curtains after a bedroom had been decorated. She teased me about growing into a young man. I'd known her since I was a small boy and still called her Aunt Liz. Questioned about my liking for girls, she kissed me and I kissed her back, using the open mouth and probing tongue technique known as

'Frenching'. Looking back, of course, Aunt Liz was feeling capricious. Alone in a bedroom with a young male, she was not the first mature female to fancy corrupting a youth. Boys should all be so lucky. She let me see her large breasts bared, to fondle and suck them, before she enquired if I had ever seen a woman's sexual parts, and would I like to?

When she lowered her knickers the sight of the crinkled outer lips splitting a plumply curved mound, won my immediate approval. Her magnificent, succulent cunt nestled in the fork of splendid strapping thighs. Allowed, indeed encouraged, to feel, sniff and stare at it, she easily persuaded me to perform oral sex on her. I found mouthing her, sucking in the lips and tonguing deeply, was so exciting that I came in my pants.

We met often after that, once or twice each week, and I made her come on my tongue. In time she sucked me off in her mouth, swallowing my emission with relish, and on occasion she let me fuck her.

But both of us were happy with our oral sessions. The smell, taste and feel of a woman's quim, the way she wriggled and moaned as she reached her orgasm during oral sex was to me the greatest thrill. She got so aroused that my face and mouth would be saturated with her vaginal juices. When I was eighteen, by then experienced in the art, I succeeded in introducing another married woman to oral sex. Her husband was in the army and had never gone down on her. Indeed she'd never heard of the act but took to loving it at every chance. Then she mentioned it to a woman who worked in the same factory as us.

This woman was also married with her husband in the forces. Getting preggy while husbands were away was the great fear at the time. Lonely, they got randy, and as word spread among a favoured few, I was in demand to provide sexual thrills with my mouth and tongue. Inevitably I fucked two of these women when they got to trust me, and I performed oral sex on a variety of women from sixteen to fifty-four.

I was well into my twenties when I met Dot, my wife-to-be. After I'd fallen for her, I remained on my best behaviour and tried nothing while courting – but let her finish this letter in praise of oral pleasure.

I thought Ray was ever so nice when we courted and he never tried to take advantage of me. A girl likes this in her fellow, but I know I often wished he *would* try something. On our honeymoon we made love two or three times a night and I loved it. I thought Ray very good at getting me excited and making me come, something I'd only ever known by my own hand or, dare I say it, a Vaselined carrot. The start of our oral relationship began after our return from our honeymoon. Tired, I was awakened one dawn by my new hubby kissing me all over. He liked us both to sleep naked and had the covers drawn back, sucking my tits and lowering his head between my legs.

Soon he began pressing kisses to my vagina and lapping his tongue up and down the outer lips. This excited me so greatly that I had a strong orgasm almost immediately, helped I'm sure by the thought of someone actually kissing me 'down there', which was almost unthinkable. He had never done this to me on our honeymoon. He told me later that he thought I'd be disgusted but the urge to do so proved stronger. I groaned and begged him to continue while his tongue darted in and out, lapped around, tickled my clitoris, and thoroughly explored every nook and cranny of my cleft. I just writhed in ecstasy and urged him to continue sucking me.

Eventually I was exhausted by the numerous wracking orgasms and my husband came up for air and lay beside me. When I stretched out a foot it got very wet and I realised he'd climaxed at the bottom of the bed while tonguing me. This told me that it excited him greatly too. The lovely sensations sent coursing through my cunt by his tongue thrilled me so much that I timidly asked him to do it to me again when he came home from work that night. I had his meal ready but, delighted I'd asked, he insisted on doing me first.

He sat me in an armchair, drew off my knickers, spread my legs and gave me a severe tonguing. Once again I had multiple orgasms. I was powerless to stop even when in torment through the intensity of the comes. He said I had a hair-trigger cunt, considering the ease in which I climaxed. Soon he showed me that when we lay reversed, head to foot in the '69' position, his erect penis was offered to my face. It was another experience for me but I soon began kissing and licking his prick and balls, ending with sucking him as he licked me. When he came, ejaculating spurts of his sperm into my mouth, I swallowed and carried on draining him until he was soft.

Then we began greedily feeding off each other, sucking and swallowing each other's juices until dry and exhausted. At least three to five times a week we indulge in oral sex, although we are now in our fifties. We are both considered very active for our age. I often wonder just how much semen I have swallowed during our marriage but I have no intention of cutting down on my intake.

Dot and Ray, Somerset

In the Family

I'm not much of a drinker and, after a friend's wedding, I drove my brother and his wife back to their house. It was obvious my brother Terry had tippled too much and, once at home, he fell asleep on the couch. His wife, Michelle, made me coffee and we drank it in the kitchen. Needless to say, she was pretty merry having had a drink at the reception and, being good-looking, had been well danced by the men there while her hubby propped up the bar.

She mentioned this, saying rather wistfully that he would be no use to her that night. 'More fool him,' I said, thinking what a fine body she had. 'Graham,' she giggled, 'you're staring at my boobs, you naughty boy.' I didn't deny it. 'Before Terry and I went off to the wedding, he had me on the bed but didn't make me come,' she said. 'That just got me worked up and now the drunken sod is no use to anybody.'

I guessed the drink and frustration had lowered her inhibitions, for Michelle had never been one to be suggestive before. However, such talk made me acutely conscious of my own erecting organ, now brazenly bulging out my trouser front. It was all too obvious to my sister-in-law. I mumbled that I'd better leave but, before I could turn to go, she grabbed me. She pressed her belly and pubic mound against my seriously throbbing prick, by then a long cylinder of bone-hard flesh.

'Let's not waste that beauty,' she whispered hoarsely, her tits crushed to my chest and her cunt rub-rubbing against my dong. I tried to prise her away, not that I wasn't eager to fuck her, but my big brother was just yards away in the other room. When I mentioned this, Michelle laughed. 'He'll be there until morning. Forget about him. Now is our chance. I'm desperate and I want your big cock in my wet pussy.'

As if to make sure of having me, she pulled aside the neck of her dress and placed my hand on her exposed tit. Her other hand crept down to my cock and she unzipped me while I stood frozen to the spot, unable to stop her. The feel of my throbber in her soft hand was ecstasy and I moaned in pleasure which made her say that since I liked it so much, why stop? 'I'll show you how a blow-job should be done and then you can fuck me,' she said.

I could hardly believe this was happening to me, but with my prick in her grasp, she suddenly leant over. First she expertly flicked her tongue over the tip, then her warm mouth slowly glided up and down the shaft. I felt my knees buckle and I held on to her head as she suctioned gluttonously on my dick. She knew I was starting to unload and sucked and swallowed as my hot spunk spurted into her throat. Standing, she then asked me to finger her as she turned and leant over the sink. She pulled up her dress, revealing her rounded buttock cheeks barely covered by her panties. 'Go on, silly, take them off,' she urged me.

A glance through into the living room showed that Terry was still flat out in a drunken stupor. Before me, his wife hoisted her bottom and, with trembling hands, I lowered her panties over her ankles. She then parted her legs, murmuring that I should feel her and play with her clit. I found her sopping wet, my fingers slipping in as she writhed her bottom. Unable to resist, I dived between her legs to lap and lick at her cunt. 'Now do me,' I heard her moan. 'I want that prick up my cunt. Don't disappoint me like your brother.'

I yanked down my trousers and entered her with one almighty push. Such is the stamina and virility of youth that I still had a cock stiff enough to penetrate a juicy quim even after being sucked off. In her position, leaning over the sink, I pushed her down until her back dipped and her arse tilted further so I was fucking her doggy-position. On tiptoe to gain depth, I felt my prick sink to the depths of her cunt, her inner muscles gripping my pistoning dick as she squealed out for me to go faster and deeper.

She had a beautiful tight cunt which gripped my prick like a velvet glove. The feel of my rampant chopper buried deep in her love-tube was indescribable, making us both groan aloud as we fucked furiously. What delighted me was that she was climaxing time after time. My own come was delayed because of shooting my load in her mouth. So I carried on humping her while she thrashed about, gyrating her arse back against me as I shafted her.

The inevitable happened, of course. My balls churned and soon I ejaculated five or six long jets of semen high into her cunt. Later, still shaking, I drove away in my car amazed at what had happened. I decided it would be a one-off, despite Michelle being such a great fuck.

Suffice to say the next celebration we attended together was for the christening of Terry and Michelle's baby daughter. When the vicar announced that the baby was a gift from God, did Michelle really look at me with a wicked gleam in her eye? Or was that just my imagination?

Graham, Barnsley

Fire Down Below

Most couples argue about sex, and in most cases it's the husband who wants to fuck more often than the wife. In my case it was the opposite. I always desired more cock than I got from Werner. He was more into his hobbies like the model railway that ran through the attic. He'd spend whole days up there, which could be handy if I was entertaining a lover. Now he's into surfing the net or whatever he does crouched over a computer every evening and weekend.

Through not getting it, I suppose, I wanted sex every night whereas Werner thought he was doing me a favour fucking me once a week. He complained we'd wear ourselves out. So can you blame me for taking every chance that came my way? Through our married years, my twenties, thirties and now my forties, while hubby failed to keep me fulfilled and satisfied, many of his friends surely did. I got more cock when Werner was in the attic or at work than ever I did when we were in bed. If you were a male pal of Werner's, you got to enjoy a fringe benefit, screwing his horny wife while he played with his toys.

What with my appetite, it was inevitable that on occasions I'd get caught. More than once my husband came home unexpectedly and caught me naked in bed with another man. But I looked after him too well in other ways for him to walk out or tell me to leave. One afternoon he caught his eighteen-year-old nephew in the bathroom with me. Jackie and I had showered together after working in the garden and I couldn't resist trying the lad out. When my husband looked in, I was bending over the washbasin with my bottom sticking out and Jackie was behind me, holding me by my tits, his young dick shunting back and forth as he strenuously fucked me from the rear.

That led to a big row. I told Werner I was fed up being married to a man who went to sleep rather than fuck. I told him he could look after himself as I was going away for a spell at his sister's boarding house by the sea. 'If you want me back,' I told him, 'you'll have to beg.' I knew he would soon be grovelling since he couldn't cope on his own.

As it was out of season, the boarding house had just one guest, an elderly gent with grey hair who was looking for a house to buy. Roland had a sense of humour and a very pleasant nature. He had been a colonel in the army.

Roland swam in the sea every morning, even in March. I noted his body was muscular and without an ounce of fat. The second morning I was there, I was making up my bed when he looked in the open door and offered to help. He said my sister-in-law and her husband had left to go shopping in Brighton, which I knew as I'd heard their car leave. They'd also said they'd be lunching there and not to expect them until tea time. I intended to stroll on the sea front, catch up on the book I was reading. As we made the bed, I thanked Roland for his help, noting he was looking at me with interest.

'You know you're beautifully built,' he observed without a trace of shyness. 'Just how a woman should look, not frail or fragile, but nicely rounded in the right places.'

‘Such as my boobs and my bottom?’ I suggested saucily to keep the old chap going. I guessed he was seventy at least. ‘Naughty you, I’ve seen you looking at me. I don’t think you could manage me.’

‘Madam,’ he said. ‘There may be snow on the roof but there’s a fire down below.’ I was still wearing my dressing robe and he was eyeing me as if to discover if I was wearing anything under it. Of course there wasn’t and I deliberately let the robe fall open at the neck, thus revealing my cleavage. He wore a tracksuit, and he made no attempt to hide the fact he had a good hard-on. The stiffy was thrusting the material way out in front. ‘I’m glad you’re going to be with us for a week or so,’ he added. ‘Hard luck for your husband, however, not having you in his bed at nights.’

‘And you wouldn’t mind taking his place while I’m staying here?’ I asked teasingly. Certain I was on safe ground, I squeezed the bulge in the front of his tracksuit pants, surprised at the thickness and iron-hard feel in my hand. ‘You’re hung like a stallion, Roly,’ I gasped. ‘Do you still remember how to use this brute?’

‘I did only this morning,’ he said meaningfully. ‘Nobody else was up but your sister-in-law when I came down to go for my swim. We had what is known as a table-ender in the kitchen.’ While telling me this about Elsa, Werner’s sister, he watched for my reaction to see if I’d be shocked. As I continued squeezing his dick, he loosened my dressing gown and eased it off my shoulders until it dropped to the carpet, leaving me naked. I was becoming aroused as his eyes devoured my body.

‘You old sod, you want to fuck me, don’t you?’ I said as he took me in his arms. My arms went about his neck and we kissed lingeringly. I really put some effort into it as our tongues entwined. I rubbed my pubic mound up and down on the bulge in his pants. When he said that I was hot, I said, 'I hoped I'd find someone to put out my fire while I'm here.'

'Don't waste time looking around, you've found him,' he laughed, laying me back on the bed we had just made and taking off his tracksuit. I had to stare in disbelief, never having known anyone whose prick was as rigidly long and thick as the awesome thing rearing before me.

It might well have struck fear into a woman less familiar with taking the cock than me. Wanting him to fuck me right there and then, I held out my arms in welcome, my breasts lifting. I also spread my thighs to give him a good look at whatever caught his fancy, my tits and cunt.

First he put his face between my thighs, his mouth clamped over my cunt and his tongue delving inside. I was about to clasp his head to keep him eating me when he slapped my thigh and said the cock was better than the tongue. Climbing up over me, he put my hand on his prick, letting me lodge it between my cunt lips. Inch by inch he did the rest, sliding it right up into me until it touched bottom.

My head was spinning, thinking about all that amount of cock going up into me. I cried out for him to fuck me harder as lust took over my brain. I wrapped my legs about his back and thrust up to his lunges. I pulled his face down to my jiggling boobs and while his solid prick moved back and forth inside me, he sucked on my nipples as if trying to draw my tits into his mouth. Knowing what men like, I screamed out that he was the best fuck I'd ever known, his prick the biggest ever taken, that he fucked me better than my husband and could fuck me anytime and anywhere!

I made it so good for him he knew he was getting a piece of ass he would remember. Mind you, not all of it was for his benefit, so mind-blowing was the feel of all that dick shafting me. I wailed as I was swept into my first climax. Still he continued to bring me to shattering orgasms as his prick lunged and shunted in my cunt passage. At last, drained by the multiple comes he was giving me, I heard his grunts as he fucked faster and felt his copious load of cream shoot deep into me.

In our final spasms we clung tightly to each other, my bottom lifting from the mattress to meet each forward shove into me while he was humping me for all he was worth before finishing. As he collapsed on top and I felt his hot breath on my cheek, I reckoned we had fucked to a draw, both shagged out. 'Did you like what we just did, Roly?' I asked teasingly on regaining my breath. 'Was that as good a fuck as you get with Elsa?'

Whether it was or not, I knew he was going to be a busy old fucker during the time I stayed there.

Lotte, Surrey

More Than One Way

I am a girl of nineteen and have been married to an older man for three months. He's always boasting about his wide experience with women and blames me if I don't climax during sex. He goes on about me being young and untrained. From my point of view, he hasn't a clue about the female anatomy, especially the clitoris. To shut him up, sometimes I fake having an orgasm, but I'm going to stop doing that. I want some real satisfaction.

Cliff's good to me in every other way and I've been reluctant to tell him what he should do to bring me off. I'd like to show him how I've had multiple orgasms before we married. If only he knew about what he thinks is his innocent little bride! To get satisfaction now, I use a secret selection of vibrators and dildoes. He thinks women should come only when being fucked by a male. That's great too, but why stop at that? Enjoy everything, I say.

I'm not a lesbian, although all of my sexual experiences were with girls and older women before I married Clifford. My parents were protective of me going with boys, but hadn't a clue about female sex. For me it started at school. From my marital experiences, I'm inclined to believe women make better lovers than men. They get pleasure from giving as well as receiving, and know the getting there is as pleasurable as arriving at an orgasm.

A woman does not want to be rushed. My latest woman friend (who is married too) visits and we play with each other, rub our pubic mounds together and masturbate with our fingers. We undress each other, fondle and kiss, paying special attention to our sensitive breasts and nipples. I must admit I find it enjoyable to let her use her mouth and tongue on my cunt, driving me to distraction when she sucks on my clitty. She has also introduced a double-dildo into our sex play and gives me multiple climaxes that way. We get pleasure from masturbating ourselves while watching each other. I'd like to bring myself off in front of my husband while he does the same. A man should like that, I'd say.

So why does the male ego require that a woman only has her climax with a cock inside her? I'm sure if men (my husband especially) played with their wives with tongue and hand more often, they would find that watching and hearing our female reactions can be most erotic. I find the idea of shouting out lewd words and being extremely wanton in bringing myself off most exciting. I'm sure there are many sex games that are just as pleasurable to men as straight fucking.

Of course I'd like to be fucked to orgasm. I love my husband's hard dick, love to rub it, hold it to my breast, suck on it in my mouth, and have thought about having it up my back passage. But let us also dismiss this idea that a woman must orgasm only during penetration by the male penis. That's fine, but men, please experiment. We *want* you to. At present, sex with my husband is a nominal grope, then a few minutes gasping and groaning with him on top of me. Then, just as I'm hoping it will continue, it's all over!

So you can see why I welcome my woman friend and

why I'm jolly well going to have to tell my husband what I'd really like!

Clifford's Wife, London

Nice Little Earner

When my husband left me I lost everything. I ended up in a crabby little bed-sit with no money. I'd have loved to be in a nice office job with a good salary but I'd married in my teens and wasn't qualified for anything. I wasn't willing to live off the social money so I did cleaning work, mostly late at night for the extra money even though that was peanuts.

I didn't miss my husband, he'd been a dead loss and as far as sex was concerned not an exciting partner. At least, I guessed that he wasn't, having no other lovers to compare him with. All I knew was sex with him was nothing to get excited about. I much preferred bringing myself off and was amazed and delighted by the strength of the climaxes I gave myself. I was sure no man could give me such pleasure.

On my way to work one night, a big expensive car stopped just ahead of me. As I made to walk past, the nearside window lowered electronically and a man leaned over from the driver's seat. 'Twenty-five,' he said mysteriously. I saw him eyeing me up and down with interest. 'Thirty then,' he added, opening the rear door by reaching over his driving seat. 'Get in if you're going to. It will have to be a quickie as I'm expected at home—'

I knew then what he wanted. He thought I was a pro looking for a client. 'I've got a condom in case you haven't,' he said. He wore glasses but was neatly dressed in a nice suit with spotless collar and tie. The idea that he was willing to pay for sex with me suddenly seemed arousing and wicked. I felt responsive palpitations in my cunt, moistness seeping as if in readiness for penetration. Getting into the rear of the car, I trembled with anticipation.

The car smelt of new leather as he lowered me back along the rear seat, fumbling under my skirt to be at my knickers and remove them. He growled *Oh yes* as he slipped a finger into my cunt and worked it about, praising me for having a nice tight juicy hole. Then he put my hand on his prick, which was rearing stiffly out of his fly. My excitement at feeling its throb and heat in my grasp made me tell him to hurry up and put it in me. 'Fuck me,' I told him because that's what I wanted. He said I was pretty hot for a pro, adding I was his first black girl.

He handed me the condom, lolling back on the seat and telling me to roll it on him. 'Wet my dick first, it goes on easier,' he suggested. 'Give a few sucks to the stalk and around the knob. Make it good and I'll add another ten.' In my mind I calculated he was offering me forty pounds, almost as much as I earned in a week at my cleaning work. I had never put a penis in my mouth although of course I knew women did and that men must love it. As I hesitated, I felt his grip on the back of my neck, pushing my head lower over his cock.

'Suck,' he said, more sharply than he'd spoken before. Tentatively, wondering how the feel and taste of a man's prick would be inside my mouth, I covered the big knob with my lips. Immediately I felt my excitement mounting: the knowledge that I was now a cocksucker was thrilling. As I angled the hard hot stalk between my tongue and the roof of my mouth it seemed the most natural thing to suck it in greedily. I felt the man shudder as he worked his hips against my face. He's fucking my mouth, I thought, and that too made me feel lewd. 'Suck me! Suck and swallow, you horny slut!' I heard my client shout as he neared his orgasm.

Then he convulsed and a gush of spunk flooded my mouth. The spasms grew weaker as his climax subsided and I swallowed the lot as he fell away from me, his diminishing cock slipping from my lips, leaving them sticky. I licked them clean with my tongue thinking the salty taste was not unpleasant. As I watched him fasten his zip, I said in disappointment, 'Aren't you going to fuck me?'

'You're an unusual whore,' he laughed. 'That made you horny, did it? Got you worked up for a screw. Most girls just take the money and run. That's another thing, you should get the money up front, *before* the action takes place. What if I refused to pay now that you've relieved me of my load?' 'Pay me now then,' I said and he opened his wallet and gave me two twenties and a ten which I put in my purse. He also handed me a card. 'Sorry but I can't fuck you, much as I'd like to,' he said, his hand squeezing my breasts. 'I'd like to see those big tits and your bare arse. This is my mobile phone number and I'll look forward to your calling me soon. We'll arrange somewhere more comfortable than a car and you'll find me most appreciative and generous. What's your name, so I'll know who's calling?'

I told him 'Rosetta' and got out of his car. Then I remembered I'd left my panties behind and wondered if he had a wife who might find them. Suddenly I noticed my boss leaning against his car further down the road. He often looked into the offices his staff cleaned just to make sure we'd turned up. When I went to speak to him, he asked me bluntly if I'd been earning a bit on the side.

I was so surprised that I became flustered and he knew at once he'd guessed right. 'I don't blame you, Rose,' he said. 'You girls are sitting on a goldmine, especially a big-titted beauty like you. I've always fancied fucking you myself. How much do you usually charge?'

I had to laugh at his cheek. 'For you, twenty pounds,' I said, my cunt still pulsing with arousal from my cocksucking session which had left me needing relief. My boss was an older man, but always clean and smart. We went into the office I was due to clean and he guided me to the biggest desk, making me bend forward over it. My skirt was raised and he expressed delight at the sight of my big bare bottom. I meekly obeyed when he told me to hollow my back and raise my behind. Trembling at the enormity of what I was doing, the thought that I was selling myself made me more turned on than I could ever remember.

'You've got a lovely arse,' I heard him say, shivering as I felt his lips brush over both cheeks. There was no way I could keep my legs together as he prised apart the cushiony spheres of my bottom and said what a lovely sight it was to look at such a luscious juicy split. He bent and began tonguing me deeply, forcing my cunt lips apart and probing, then sucking at my clitoris. 'What a nice tight quim to lick,' he muttered. 'It's just made to fuck.'

'Then *fuck* it!' I screamed out shamelessly, desperate to get his prick up me. Glancing around I saw it in his hand, a fine sturdy specimen of engorged tubular flesh. I tilted my arse higher and waggled it at him as a come-on, remembering how the man in the car had shot his creamy hot spunk to the back of my throat. Now I wanted a similar load jetted up my burning cunt to drench the fire there.

Although I was a comparatively inexperienced whore, it seemed natural to grip my boss's pistoning prick with my cunt muscles as he plunged into me ever deeper. I groaned and urged him on as he drove into my sopping cunt. 'Fuck me. Fuck me. That's what I want – a good fucking!' I shouted as he eased my bottom to the edge of the desk so that my rear-directed cunt was more conveniently positioned for full penetration. Rising on tiptoe, he repeatedly went into me with his balls thudding against the underside of my bum cheeks.

In the throes of coming, I heard him growling obscenities about me in his mounting excitement. 'Take that, you slut! What a horny bitch you are, Rose, a right little whore!' This only added to the arousal I felt at being shafted by his dick. 'Fuck me like the slut I am then!' were the words I used to answer him as I thrust my bottom back against his belly. We fucked so frenziedly that our efforts moved the desk along the floor. It seemed I was being jolted by one long continuing come as his prick erupted like a volcano, pouring hot Iava into my soft and receptive slit.

'I've put enough in you to make a dozen babies,' he said as we recovered our senses. One was enough, for within weeks it was obvious he had put me in the family way. That's how I became a partner in his office cleaning business, by marrying the boss. He insisted we marry, however, before he learned I was pregnant by him. When he proposed he said I was the best fuck he'd ever known and didn't want to lose me. There's been more romantic marriage offers, I'm sure, but I knew what he meant. It was fate when he saw me getting out of the car on that night and thought I was on the game. For the first and last time.

Rosetta, Leeds

3. Any Time At All

My Cheating Heart
Begging For It
French Lessons
Ex-Rated Treatment
What a Night
Bigger and Better
Late-Night Shopping
On the Menu
Like Mother, Like Daughter
Pregnant Pause
Blowing the Whistle

My Cheating Heart

Sex with my husband Joe became fantastic after I discovered he was having an affair. It made me aroused hearing him talk about what he did with the married woman he slept with – just thinking about it got me feeling hot. That made me want him to make love to me as often as possible, changing me into a real sexpot. I couldn't get enough.

This abrupt change in my sexual appetite delighted my husband. A woman doctor friend who I told about this, said that I was reclaiming my territory and letting Joe know that my cunt was the only place where his prick should go. Or between your breasts, in your mouth or even up your bottom if you like a bit of vice-versa, she laughed, advising me to be as sexy as I liked.

One result of making advances to Joe and being so demanding was that now he didn't need other women. We'd been married eighteen years and he was forty to my thirty-seven. Joe is a self-made businessman in the building trade and a rough diamond. I am a college graduate and school teacher and our one son is at boarding school. Joe had given me an easy life with no financial worries, yet our sex life had dwindled to no body contact and separate beds.

Then his affair came out, the woman's husband coming to our house and making a scene. He kept shouting that Joe had been with her. 'You fucked my wife, you bastard! Our cleaning lady caught the pair of you naked in bed in my house, you swine! And what was she doing to you in your car?' I found that listening to these lurid details of what my husband had been up to with his lover, had the surprising result of making me strangely excited.

The thrills I experienced pulsated down to my vagina, making it throb and ache, releasing inner juices that I knew were certain signs of arousal. I felt weak at the knees, shocked at my reaction, but could not deny I felt wonderfully wanton and randy. Joe told the man if he'd not been fucking his wife satisfactorily, it was no surprise that she'd gone elsewhere. When the man had stamped out, Joe told me his affair really was over, but that I was to blame as well for keeping my legs shut and never giving him a ride as a wife should.

I could have said I felt like a good ride then, but was too shy to say what I wanted. In bed that night my hands fondled my breasts and plucked at my nipples as I aroused myself, something I'd not done since my teenage years. As my lust mounted and I got beyond caring about shame, one hand went between my thighs and stroked the moistened lips of my cunny. All the time I was recalling what the angry man had said about my husband and his wife pleasuring themselves.

Then I knew I would need to climax, such was my desperation. It struck me, why should I masturbate when a perfectly horny husband was in bed in the next room. Getting out of bed I pulled off my nightie, going nude to knock on his door. 'Come in,' he said, sitting up in the dark. 'I'll see you get a divorce. Don't worry, I'll always see you and our lad gets well looked after.' Then he put on his bedside lamp, seeing me full-frontal naked. 'God, you always did have great tits,' he said admiringly. 'Tits and arse, the best I've ever seen. Are you trying to torment me?'

'No, tempt you,' I said. 'Tell me what that woman was doing bent over you in your car. Tell me everything you did to her. I want to hear. Shall I get in bed beside you while you tell me?' In answer he drew back the duvet, and sleeping naked as he always did, with great satisfaction I saw he already had a rearing erection. 'Fuck me with that like you did to her,' I heard my voice say hoarsely. 'Do all the things the pair of you did.

That was how our marathon sex sessions began as I learnt to enjoy doing all the sexy things Joe and the woman had engaged in. I found his detailed descriptions of their lewd romps extremely erotic, becoming so aroused as to do whatever he described: sucking, titty-fucking, dog-fashion – as well as the wickedly improper rear entry. He asked me to tell him of my sexual adventures, but as I'd had none he suggested I invented some worthy of recounting to him in our sex games.

It was he who on a holiday in Mauritius practically threw me together with a Frenchman. Jean picked me up at the bar at our hotel, propositioned me and, with Joe making himself scarce, took me to his house and fucked me several times during our stay. On our return, I went out with a colleague from school who had long made known his desire for me. Divorced, with a flat near the school, he undressed me and took me to bed weekly. On leaving the flat after hours of fucking and sucking, my husband would be parked nearby waiting to take me home, eager to hear every detail of our orgies.

Often when we make love after my being with another man – and there have been more than a few in the intervening years – Joe wants me to pretend he's the other guy. I call him by the name of my present lover and beg him to fuck me because my husband can't, all of which arouses us both tremendously. I look back to when my life was devoid of sex and say it has only become such a thrill because my husband was a cheat.

Susan, Reading

Begging For It

Widowed for seven years, I still had occasional urges for sex but could do little about it except masturbate using my fingers. I did fancy trying some of the things I'd seen advertised in a magazine, shown to me by a friend who was complaining of the filth her husband read in secret. 'He's sex mad, always wanting me,' she moaned, and I felt like telling her how lucky she was. As for the magazine, I couldn't get the address of the company who sold sex toys as it would have been impossible to ask her to show me. I probably wouldn't have had the nerve to send for a vibrator or dildo anyway.

I was in my early fifties, comfortably off and was still quite presentable, I believed. And so I booked a holiday in Tunisia, hopeful of finding a willing male in the same hotel. It was far enough away for it not to matter if I had to act the tart to show I was available. I arrived at a lovely hotel with a golden stretch of beach before it. Everything was perfect except that the hotel was filled either with married couples or single women like myself.

I made friends with Alice, a woman of about my own age, and we'd take coffee together or walk on the beach among the fishing boats dragged up on the sand. I learned she was a widow like myself, the wife of a vicar. One night after dinner, I was surprised when she slipped away without explanation, for we usually sat on the verandah admiring the velvet black night and the bright stars in the sky. Alone, I was about to return to my room to read, when I caught a glimpse of my friend making for the beach. She had a shawl over her head and was hurrying along as if not wanting to stop.

We'd been told it was perfectly safe to wander around the vicinity of the hotel during the day, but what of night? And where was my new friend going so secretively? I plucked up courage, urged on by curiosity, and followed at a distance. Alice walked around several beached fishing boats which made it easy for me to follow her without detection. Then I saw her stop and a young local man appeared from behind one of the boats. In the starlit night, my eyes now used to the dark, I recognised the youth as one of the Arab lads who sold souvenirs outside the hotel.

Whatever is Alice doing meeting him here on this deserted beach and at this time of night? I stupidly asked myself. Watching from behind the hull of a nearby boat, I saw the young Arab spread a blanket on the sand. Then to my amazement the woman and the youth clasped each other eagerly and began to exchange kisses. I was shocked but found myself becoming aroused. I saw Alice throw aside her shawl, kick off her sandals, then draw her dress over her head.

Alice had come prepared to meet her lover. She was naked, her skin silvery in the starlight, her big breasts pendulous and sex delta shaved bare. As she lay back, the youth went from kissing her mouth to her breasts, then on down to between her spread thighs where he began to kiss and tongue her vulva. I plainly saw her hands pulling and tugging his head as he pleasured her that way, could see her hips begin to jerk and heard her keening and whining in ecstasy.

The lad then knelt up before her and pulled off his

robe to appear as naked as she was. His penis reared and I saw Alice take it in her hand, then lean forward and cover it with her lips.

It was something I'd never done – put a penis in my mouth. I'd heard about the act, of course, and in my fantasising I'd thought I'd like to do it. I'd once shyly suggested it to my husband but he thought it distasteful. But I wanted to do it right now – and have my cunt licked out like Alice. My thighs became sticky and my knickers damp as I began to lubricate freely. I badly wanted to masturbate.

Then the youth got on top of Alice. I saw her legs circle his back and her hands pull on his buttocks as her bottom lifted jerkily from the blanket. She was undoubtedly being deeply penetrated. The youth's bare buttocks heaved as he thrust into her and again I heard her whining and sighing in bliss. You sneaky thing, I told myself angrily, envious that she'd been bold enough to seek out a lover. That he was so handsome and young only added to my resentment. He was virile too. I could tell from the way he lunged into his partner, bringing squeals of pleasure from her lips as she urged him on.

What surprised me was that the mild Alice began to use crude words, ordering him loudly to *fuck her*, *fuck her hard*, *fuck her cunt* and *keep making her come*. I knew from his sales pitch outside the hotel that his English was limited, but it was evidently good enough to know what she'd said. In turn he vowed he'd *fuck her*, *fuck her good* and *fill her up with spunk*. Ah, but again this was something I'd wished I could have said to my husband and he to me during our rather dismal bouts of intercourse. *Go on, fuck Alice silly*, *ram it up her greedy cunt*, I thought. I could barely stop myself from shouting out to encourage the lusty youth.

He rolled aside after both had gone into long orgasmic spasms. Lying together, they talked and exchanged kisses until Alice put on her dress and shawl and made her way back to the hotel. I followed and went to bed full of wonder at what I'd seen. I wished the youth had been doing those things to me and couldn't sleep until I made myself come through self-pleasuring.

At breakfast next morning I sat and looked at Alice in a new light. I followed her that night and saw them making love again. The following day she left for home.

For me, it was now make-or-break time.

The boy sold brass objects like ashtrays and little Arabic coffee pots. His wares were laid out on a blanket – probably the same one he used to lay down on the sand before having sex with Alice. Nervously, I sounded him out. Not being bold enough to ask him to meet *me* on the beach at night, I asked if he still had some paintings by a local artist that I'd seen him selling the day I'd arrived. 'Will get, will bring them to your room when I get them this afternoon,' he said, the ghost of a smile on his lips as if he knew something.

I spent the morning at the pool, took lunch, then noted he was not at his pitch. Going up to my room, I paced nervously, now sorry I had approached him. It was incredibly hot. Soon there was a knock on my door and I opened it to find the boy standing there with several paintings of desert scenes. He lined them up against the wall of my room and sat back on the bed to await my verdict. I selected one I really liked. As I went for my purse to pay him, he asked if that was all I really wanted?

Flustered, I asked him what he meant. 'I saw you follow your friend down to the beach at night when she came to meet me,' the boy said. 'If you want the same for yourself, I would like very much to be your lover. You are a very beautiful lady.'

Whether I believed him or not, it was nice to hear it said, and indeed the young man was eyeing me like he really meant it. With my stomach in turmoil, I locked the door of my room and with trembling hands began to lower my knickers. 'All, like Alice,' I heard him say gently, seeing the youth before me undressing. He showed me his long, thick, circumcised penis which reared up before his flat brown belly. He took the hem of my summer dress and drew up over my head, throwing it aside and leaving me wearing only my bra.

'*Please*,' I said weakly, but he was already behind me, unclipping the hooks and letting the bra fall away from my breasts. Then his hands slid around my body, the palms cupping my fleshy mounds, seductively squeezing and fondling them, his fingers plucking my nipples. In the long mirror before me I saw myself naked and found it thrilling to watch myself being fondled while I felt the rigid rod of his penis pressing into the cleave of my buttocks. 'Take me! Oh dear, did I say that?' I heard myself moan. He laid me gently on my back across the bed and leant down to nuzzle and kiss my breasts, sucking greedily on both nipples in turn.

Arousal surging through my body, I welcomed his hand going between my legs and stroking the inside of my thighs. His fingers entered my vagina, exploring the moist inner walls and brushing my clitoris. Squeaking with excitement, I clasped his rampant manhood, traitorously thinking that its size put my poor late husband's cock to shame. Well aroused by now, with the steamy scent of my cunt filling the room, I shameless begged the boy to *fuck* me, finding it natural to use the word in my urgent need.

'I will fuck you in good time, when you will beg even more,' he smirked into my face, going down between my spread thighs and delving his tongue inside my hot soaked channel to stroke my sensitive clitoris. Helplessly I arched my back and thrust my crotch into his face, screeching as he brought me to the most wracking climax I'd ever known. While still in its throes, jerking out of control, his strong young hands forced my thighs wide. Then he was in me, penetrating me to the hilt. The feel of his huge throbbing stalk in my hole was out of this world.

Shouting, humping my bottom from the bed, I told him to *fuck, fuck, fuck* me silly. Soon I was coming as if electric shocks were jolting through me while he pistoned into me. All too soon I felt his sturdy cock jerk and twitch, heard his strangled cry as he pumped his hot juice deep inside me. As I subsided and he rolled apart from me, I thought that this must be the most heavenly way to spend an afternoon. We showered together – another first for me – then he regained his erection and fucked me again, up against the tiled wall of the bathroom.

I still had ten days holiday left, during which time he had me as often and as much as he liked. Being of Middle Eastern extraction, he had his own special desires, one of which was a liking for anal intercourse. I was taken this way and soon found this rear-entry penetration highly pleasurable. I've no doubt that he serviced quite a few lonely middle-aged women like myself and satisfied us all with his large endowment and youthful virility. Enough to say North Africa is now my regular holiday venue. Naughty me, three times this year so far. I write this on behalf of sexually active widows like myself, to say we are still available.

Rose, Stafford

French Lessons

It's years ago now, but the memory of Beatrice Cole will always remain fresh. I was a senior approaching my seventeenth birthday at a well-known public school, cramming to take the Sandhurst exam for a career in the Army. Big for my age and a regular in the rugby squad, my academic and behaviour record was not good.

Like all the other pupils in an all-boys' school, I was randy and frustrated, girls and sex monopolising my thoughts. I was no virgin, having screwed a few girls in my home village and an older kitchen maid working in a local hotel. The fact she was mature and married added greatly to my enjoyment of shagging her. Dodging out of school in the dark of an evening to meet her as she came off duty, getting her to bare her tits for me to suck and play with, allowing me to fuck her up against the rear wall of the hotel, confirmed me as a voracious womaniser.

Back at school Mrs Beatrice Cole, French tutor and wife of the maths teacher, was the only woman available for us boys to lust after. Twice the age of us horny lads, she was worth the adulation, being a prime thirty-four and superbly built. Her magnificent tits bulged under the silk blouses she wore and the plump cheeks of her lovely rounded bum contoured the tight skirts she always wore. We boys were sure she flaunted her goodies to arouse us and we liked to think she would gloat over the idea of us masturbating over her – which we did, regularly.

I walked behind her every chance, the bounce and wiggle of such luscious fleshy buttocks making me want to grab and fondle them. To see her breasts and bottom bared became an ardent wish, if an impossible one. Following her around the school one afternoon between lessons, she turned around to face me. 'Just what's so fascinating that you always seem to be watching me, Fulton?' she snapped, scaring me rigid.

I mean how could I blurt out that I thought her tits and arse the most beautiful things in the world? Then she laughed at my dumbstruck face and said in a teasing voice that I was a silly boy; she could guess why I watched her and that I was rather naughty. Then she walked off. I was certain she'd enjoyed taunting me and was proud of her large breasts and curvy bottom – especially the effect her assets had on us teenage pupils.

That winter I sprained my ankle badly and was confined to the dormitory on a bleak Saturday afternoon while the whole school was out watching our rugby team. Left alone, flipping through one of the girlie mags that circulate secretly among the boys, I was gently stroking my dick into a nice big erection when the door opened and Mrs Cole entered. Dressed in a scarf and heavy winter coat, she advanced to my bedside carrying a paper bag which she said contained some toffees to cheer me up.

The sight of her did that better than anything else, but I was flustered and red-faced, as I gripped the girlie mag, the bedcover tented with my hard-on.

She shook her head in amusement and took the magazine from my hand. Then she sat down in the chair beside my bed. Outside a loud cheer echoed from the rugger pitch. She said I was no doubt frustrated at not being able to play and, as if by chance, rested a hand on the bedcover directly over my rampant prick.

My helpless response was to moan with pleasure and my dick twitched and gave little jerks against her hand. To my joy and great surprise, Mrs Cole actually gave my hard-on a squeeze. 'How very stiff that feels,' she said, her voice suddenly low and hoarse. 'It must be quite painful. Do you want to relieve it? Would you like me to go?'

It had to be now or never. Plucking up nerve and courage, I said in a voice as shaky as hers that I would prefer her to do it, not forgetting to add a heartfelt *please*! With a trembling hand she began to draw back the bedcover and, at that moment, I realised she was as horny as me. Uncovered, my dick thrust up out of my pyjamas proudly, a good thick rigid length which Mrs Cole seized in her warm hand.

I did not intend to be a passive subject. Reaching forward in my sitting-up position, I curled my right arm around her and, as she turned her face to me, I clamped my lips over hers. In response her wide wet mouth opened and returned my kiss passionately, our tongues probing in the long embrace. My left hand slipped inside her coat and met a large pliant mound of prime tit which I at once fondled and squeezed. 'Please. Let me see your breasts,' I murmured as we kissed, our hot breath mixing.

Wordlessly she threw her coat off her shoulders and began undoing the buttons at the front of her blouse. As it parted, her big luscious teats were revealed, barely contained within her straining bra. While I sat transfixed, she reached behind her back to loosen the bra's fasteners and let the lacy cups fall forward. Such was the firmness of her truly magnificent boobs that, despite their fullness and size, they thrust towards me high and tilted.

'What you are asking of me is very naughty,' she said as if reproaching me. 'It must never be known if you want it to continue.' By mentioning it continuing, I took it to mean that there would be other times and I swore secrecy. I found my head drawn forward in the crook of her left arm while her right hand cupped her right breast and guided its tautly swollen nipple directly to my eager lips. I sucked greedily on the nipple, my face buried in the smooth flesh.

I suckled ecstatically on both bubs in turn, while she cooed her pleasure, smoothed my hair and cuddled me to her like a baby. Then her soft sighs turned to moans and she began shifting and grinding her bottom in her chair and it thrilled me to think she was bringing herself off. Sure enough, she uttered stifled groans and shook bodily, pushing me from her breast as her spasms subsided. I begged her to let me continue sucking on her teats, at the same time gloating that I'd made the sexy slut come.

'No,' she said weakly as my mouth sought to go back to the nipple. 'You've made them sore. Can't your just look at them.' To give prominence to their ripeness, and indeed they seemed bigger after my strenuous suckling, she sat back in the chair, her blouse wide open and her tits thrust forward. Her erect nipples glistened with my saliva and looked sucked red raw. Her right hand now went back to clutch at my engorged prick, giving it a fond squeeze and beginning to rub it gently with her cool fingers.

'I suppose it's still painful,' she said, her voice husky, enjoying no doubt the pleasant afterglow of a strong climax. 'Shall I give it relief?' *Yes, yes*, I muttered as she began a delightful rub-rub on my stalk, uncapping the knob as my dick grew even more rigid under the stroking. I lolled back in a state of bliss, my hips jerking and feeling the hot jism ready to erupt from my balls. From my face, she knew when I was about to explode and ceased suddenly to wank me, clasping my rammer limply and keeping me on the brink.

'Don't stop! Keep rubbing it!' I ordered harshly. 'Make me come!'

'No, there'd be a mess,' she said. 'There is another way. Has it ever been sucked?'

I'd only read about that delight in schoolboy handwritten porno. To my intense joy she nursed my upright stander between her ample tits, moving her shoulders up and down with it trapped in a tunnel of flesh. Another moment and I'd have drenched her neck with spunk but she deftly lowered her mouth and took my dick between her lips, at once sucking greedily and drawing my whole length in. Soon jet after hot jet of my pent-up excitement spattered to the back of her throat, all of which she gulped and swallowed readily.

Over the following months life at school certainly improved as Mrs Cole and I met secretly and as often as possible. Her husband couldn't have been doing his stuff, I reckoned, for she was always agreeable to our meeting, more often than not suggesting it herself by notes slipped in my French exercise books after marking. Under cover of winter's darkness we fucked in the sports pavilion, in her car, even in her house in the school grounds with hubby out teaching night school in town.

Every young lad should have such an eager tutor to make him sexually aware. Beatrice loved dirty talk during sex and I'd tell her my horny young dick was going to fuck her rigid, put a baby in her belly, although that wasn't a danger as she was on the pill. She liked to hear that, all the same, telling me in the heat of a fuck to make her preggy and do her husband's job for him. When in her mouth, I'd call her a cocksucking bitch and she'd tell me to fuck her mouth, shoot it all down her throat! She loved having her tits sucked and flaunted herself naked for me proudly on the evenings I went to her house while her husband was absent. How could I ever forget her? What lad ever would?

I was to find out later that there were a few boys, pupils at the school before me, who had had reason to be grateful to her as well. Years later when in the army, a colleague found out we'd been to the same boarding school. 'Did you have a French tutor called Mrs Cole?' he enquired.

Not sure what to say, I nodded. He grinned and said she was noted for her big tits and fondness for corrupting sixth-formers, if they should be so lucky! My new friend, a major, proudly announced he'd fucked her on his sixteenth birthday, the first of many screws over the next months. His older brother before him at the school had also enjoyed her favours and told him about it. Such cases do get found out and sometimes even end in court, but the generous Mrs Cole evidently got away with her hobby over the years. Good for her.

J.F., Warminster

Ex-Rated Treatment

My new husband has proved so hopeless in bed that I've turned to my ex-husband to get sexual satisfaction. My frustration came about when, even after a year of marriage, my hubby still suffered from premature ejaculation. Sometimes he even shot his load during foreplay. Fucking and oral sex with my ex had always been good. Although he now had a girlfriend, he was so keen on his nookie that I was sure he wouldn't refuse me.

I went to his house one Saturday afternoon when my husband was miles away at a football match. I knocked on the door and got no answer. Shading my eyes and looking in a window through a chink in the curtains, I saw my ex with a naked female on a rug before a blazing fire. From my point of view, I could see her broad arse facing me with his head beneath it. No doubt she was giving him a blow job at the other end while he was eating her quim. I envied her, knowing they were enjoying a full '69' – just like I used to have with him prior to being fucked by his big prong.

As if to increase my agony, he fastened his mouth over her pouchy cunt and tongue-fucked her until I could see she was delirious with pleasure. Just the thought of getting my end away like that again made my quim pulsate and drool. Feeling myself getting wetter, alone in his garden and hidden from the road by the hedge, I slipped my fingers into my knickers and rubbed my clit. Groaning, uncaring what I was doing, I finger-fucked myself until I was jerking like a puppet as the surge of a tremendous orgasm shook me rigid.

As soon as I arrived home I made a call to my ex. Right away I told him I'd called at his house, and had seen him through the window with his girlfriend, sucking and fucking. He laughed and said I should have just walked in and joined them. 'Wouldn't your girlfriend have objected to that?' I asked.

'Not Mel,' he laughed. 'She's into threesomes and orgies. I've told her you were quite a prude at times. You didn't like to admit you loved my dick in your mouth as well as your snatch. Mel would love to see you with your thighs spread wide and my stiff prick shafting in and out of your hot little twat. What did you get up to while watching us at it? Don't tell me you brought yourself off with your hand?'

As always, my ex loved to humiliate me for his amusement. I was made to admit I had masturbated, and that my reason for calling him was because my husband didn't satisfy me as he used to. Much as it shamed me to say these things, I found it very arousing too. He asked what time my husband returned home and, when I said not for several hours, he ordered me to my get arse over to him quick. While telling me this, I could hear Mel, his girlfriend, laughing in the background. Hating myself for my weakness, all the same I got back in my car and drove to his house.

There I found Mel as keen as my ex to kiss and undress me, both of them fondling my breasts and bottom. Naked, I felt powerless to stop them as he sucked on my nipples and her fingers got busy between my legs. The way she taunted me for being so wet added to my shame, and she even smacked me sharply several times on my bottom to get me to kneel down for Terry, who was standing by with his rampant cock ready to be fed into my mouth by her hand.

After I had sucked him for some time, she ordered him to fuck me. Turning me onto my hands and knees on the rug, again it was she who directed his monster into me, this time in my cunt. She grabbed my hair and twisted my face around, demanding to know what it was like for me. At the beginning of a climax, excited by Mel's domineering attitude, I gasped out that it was so big and hard, that I loved it thrusting right up my cunt, and that he was going to make me come.

That must have been obvious as I croaked out my pleasure and jerked like a person being jolted by electric shocks. My climax seemed to go on and on, several merging into one as Terry thrust into me long and hard. I had never known myself be so highly aroused and I yelled out for him to fill me, shoot into me and give me a baby – something he'd refused to do when married to me. 'It would cramp my style,' he'd say. Now I was the wife of another man he obviously thought different. I felt him throbbing and jerking deep inside me as he drenched my farthest recess with his hot seed.

After that, it became a regular thing to join Terry and Mel in a threesome and at home I became a far more contented wife. My husband was delighted that I'd settled down, glowing with pride when my extended stomach showed my pregnant state to the world. I think of going to meet Terry and Mel as no more than satisfying a physical need. I look upon it as therapy.

Joyce, Nottingham

What a Night

We argued all the way to my firm's office party and by the time we arrived Steve and I had made ourselves hoarse by screaming at each other. As my fiancé, Steve was invited as my partner, and he'd arrived at my home to pick me up in his car. At once he started to complain about what I wore – or what I wasn't wearing, according to him. With a low-cut neckline and the skirt of my dress up to my thighs, he accused me of showing off my tits and said my legs were barely covered by the scanty briefs I had on.

He said that, at nearly thirty years old, I should show more decorum and my mother, who was visiting at the time, of course agreed with him. But I'm no stick insect and Steve adored my curves. Now it seemed they were for his eyes only.

'If you got it, flaunt it,' I said.

'She's as good as showing all she's got. You'll have to take a firm hand with her,' my mum shouted as I stamped out to his car.

On drawing up at the hotel, I marched ahead of him, heading for the bar and getting wolf whistles from work colleagues who seemed to appreciate the mini-dress which was causing all the bother.

I drank several vodkas and orange, feeling tipsy and wicked as Steve took my elbow and suggested we leave before I made a fool of myself. The men who had surrounded me at the bar had been dragged off by their wives and girlfriends, one of whom called me 'a whore' to my face. 'Fuck off, you fat cow,' I'd told her, which was when Steve gave up on me and said he was leaving. 'Go then,' I said, casting my eye around to see who was available. The only one not paired off was Justin, the office junior, shy and quiet, the butt of much teasing by the female staff.

'This is your lucky day, Justin,' I told him as I grabbed him for a dance. After a spell of disco music the D.J. put on some slow smoochy stuff. Poor Justin, I noted he tried to avoid staring down into my cleavage, a creamy deep furrow dividing lots of rounded tit-flesh. He also seemed to back away from me so I cupped my palms over his bum cheeks to pull him close. With my breasts flattened to his chest and our pubic areas jammed together, I discovered the reason for his hanging back.

I felt a very stiff and substantial willy pressing up against the curved mound of my puss. At once I began to move my hips wickedly as we danced – in effect rubbing that rigid young dong up and down against the groove of my sex. My cunt began to throb for real contact, to have that teenage dick enter my rapidly juicing channel. I danced Justin to a doorway leading to a corridor. As my arms circled his neck, he crushed his mouth to mine, his tongue probing as we kissed and clung.

'I've always wanted to kiss you,' he whispered as if in ecstasy between kisses, pinning me to the wall of the passageway, his hard cock jerking against my quim.

'Then how would you like to fuck me?' I asked, as breathless as I was. Nodding eagerly in reply, he opened a door nearby and found an empty room complete with a double bed. I unzipped his trousers and pulled them down along with his pants. To my delight his randy willy popped up from under his shirt. Hot and throbbing in my hand, it looked a good seven inches of solid flesh. I want *that*, I heard myself groan feebly. Tearing at my frock to drag it over my head, I urged him to undress too.

When I stood naked before him, he just stared, his first naked female proving the stuff boys' fantasies are made of. He muttered how gorgeous my breasts were and, as I lay across the bed with legs parted to receive his dick, he leaned over to suck my tits, drawing a nipple deep into his mouth. At the same time his finger went into my soaking honeypot, squelching loudly as he explored my juicy quim and, whether by accident or design, brushing my clitty. 'If you won't fuck me, I'll fuck you,' I said savagely, desperate for the dick in me as I rolled him over and straddled his body.

Poised above his crotch, I felt the egg-shaped tip of Justin's prick pressing against my oiled pussy lips. With a downward thrust I impaled myself on his stalk, even as he grabbed my hips and began heaving up into me. With tits swinging like bells in his face, I rode him in ecstasy, changing my angle of entry as I squirmed down on his cock. Soon I was crying out for him to *fuck me*, *fuck me harder* as his bottom bumped up from the bed. His shunting prick threatened to pierce my belly as he screwed me with all the vigour of his pent-up youth. 'More, more,' I urged him, writhing in one long orgasm.

Even after being aware of his increased jerking as red hot seed was squirted into me, I urged him to keep fucking. As I finally accepted that his bolt was shot and his shrinking dick was no longer able to stay within me, I felt hands pulling me off Justin. A moment later I was being laid on my back on the bed, with a work colleague sticking his prick into me. Looking over his shoulder, I saw other men awaiting their turn, two of them stationed by the door in case their wives came looking for them. The man on top of me was muttering that he'd always wanted to fuck me. I heard the watching men urge him on, crying 'Fuck the bitch silly', 'Screw the arse off her' and other obscenities that only increased my excitement.

One by one I was shagged by as many as five members of staff, none of them lasting long as they pounded into my red-hot pussy and brought me to repeated comes in my wanton state. Alone at last, I was trying to dress myself when Justin returned to say he had got a taxi waiting outside. Having lost the nerve to return to the party, I sat in the taxi with Justin. Outside my apartment building I kissed him when he solemnly thanked me and said I had taken his virginity. Sobering up and wanting sleep, I dragged myself up to my flat to find Steve waiting there with a face like thunder.

'I made an exhibition of myself,' I told him, hurrying past to shower off the sweat and sluice out the gooey load of spunk that had been shot into me. When I returned, refreshed and in a towelling robe, I said I realised I'd been out of order and had no intention of returning to work – not if Steve was going to marry me. It was what he'd always wanted, since he was well enough off to keep me in style. Little did he know my decision was made because I dared not show my face back at the office again.

Mind you, from a woman's point of view, weren't the men who took advantage of me every bit as bad as I was? Anyway, I decided it was time to settle down and start a family as my mother and Steve wanted. As a single girl of thirty, I'd had a good run, with plenty of boyfriends, even a girlfriend and had ended it with an orgy I knew in time I would look back on with amusement. I'd also taken a sweet young man's virginity in the process. It had been some night.

Stella, Chertsey

Bigger and Better

Having only ever had intercourse with my husband, I'd never really known what I was missing when it came to sex. I'd been happily married to Roger for over twenty years. I'd been brought up in a sheltered way, with sex a taboo subject. My husband's upbringing was similar and he was anything but highly sexed. Still, three children had been made by our infrequent lovemaking even though I had never had an orgasm.

Maybe, as they say, what you don't have you don't miss. Or, rather, you settle for what you've got. I enjoyed what sex we did have, often feeling like complaining when Roger left me frustrated by finishing off quickly. I also wished he would play with my breasts sometimes and suck on my nipples. In my darker thoughts I even wondered what it would be to have my pussy sucked and licked, although I was sure that was the height of perversion. Then, some time ago, I was invited to visit a friend of my schooldays who had long ago moved to San Francisco.

With Roger's blessing, I flew to the States and was met by Georgina. She had matured well over the intervening years, and had developed into an older model of the school sports champion I'd had a crush on as a teenager. In her apartment that evening we were joined by several women friends of hers who wanted to meet me. What a jolly crowd, I thought, enjoying myself with the buffet food and perhaps overdoing the drink. It was then that one of the women suggested we view the rude videos she had brought.

I'd heard of well-endowed men, of course, but my husband's cock was average size and all I'd ever laid eyes on. On the television screen, as the lewd stories unfolded, I saw men with equipment for servicing women that I wouldn't have believed. There were cocks on display that looked over ten inches long and as thick as my wrist; all of them eagerly taken in the mouth or pussy by the women on screen. The sight of such male endowment, especially one huge black cock, aroused me greatly and made me become wet between my legs.

I wondered what it would be like to take such a big cock inside me. Georgie was watching me, no doubt guessing I was aroused. 'That black guy's monster dick has impressed you,' she said. Watching a slim girl's vagina being filled by the man's huge cock, I nodded and wistfully told Georgie how marvellous it must feel to have all that hard flesh inside. I was then asked if I'd really like a big one to fuck me, the use of the word surprising me.

All the same I nodded, too aroused to be falsely modest. One of the women present handed Georgie what I saw with shock was a perfectly formed replica of the penis, as lifelike as possible with bulbous knob and veiny stalk. It looked at about a foot long and with a girth to match its fearsome length. 'It's for you if you want it, Gwen,' Georgie offered. 'Don't be shy, all of us here use vibrators and dildos. Why don't you enjoy whatever fantasy you like while watching more videos?'

I politely declined and she did not press me. As the

drink was consumed the party got merrier and the women began to dance together. They got quite passionate in their embracing, rubbing bodies together, kissing lingeringly and occasionally changing partners. It struck me I'd obviously been invited to a meeting of gay women, and it was not long before all around me began to undress and grope each other. What with the lewd video action and what was going on in the room, my arousal heightened and my quim was pulsing to be fucked. By clenching my buttock muscles and squeezing my bum I could even hear my juices noisily squelching. In truth I longed to finger myself to gain relief.

The sight of two beautiful women sucking each other off to a climax almost at my feet was too much. As Georgie sat on the arm of my chair and kissed my neck, murmuring that I was not to feel shame, that the women around me were married too, I gave up. 'Do what you like with me, Georgie,' I moaned. 'Use that dildo to fuck me with, just make me come.' I felt her lips crush against mine and her tongue enter my mouth. Some of the other women stood around watching, which turned me on, as Georgie began to take off my clothes.

Lolling back in the deep armchair, my breasts fondled and sucked until I was almost screaming for relief, I was ready and even eager to allow anything. Georgie had hold of the big dummy prick, kneeling on the floor and telling me to open my legs wide. Someone eased a cushion under my bum, which tilted me forward and made my cunt more accessible. At once Georgie began to kiss and lick my outer lips, her tongue infiltrating inside to flick around my clit.

'Georgie, fuck me with that thing!' I screeched, brought to near delirium with my need for relief. I watched in anticipation as she slid the egg-sized knob up and down my cleft. The bulbous head was soon glistening with my copious juices. Then slowly, deliberately, she pushed forward and the huge helmet parted the outer lips and began to force a passage into my cunt. 'She's tight,' I heard a watcher, murmur, 'such a narrow entrance to her quim. Be careful, Georgie.'

'Go on,' I ordered through gritted teeth, desperate to take the replica prick inside me. 'Push harder, shove it all up!' Gradually it was worked up my cunt. My thighs widened to allow room for this monster as it slid inside me and I grunted as I swallowed the full twelve inches in my cunt. My breath camc in a series of croaks, changing to low moans and whimpers of pleasure as I grew accustomed to the mass and length inside me.

Sensing this, Georgie began to shunt the big dildo in and out of me, using long strokes and tantalising me by withdrawing it to the hilt and making me beg her to shove it up again. I implored her to go on fucking me. Soon my pelvis was thrusting back and forth as she increased the pace. I was demented by lust, with orgasms wracking my whole frame, my bottom pounded the seat of the armchair.

'Harder, deeper!' I cried out. 'Fuck every inch up me!' Georgie obliged and my climaxes continued until I was completely sated and drained of energy. Then I lay back in the chair to recover. The dildo was withdrawn from my quim, glistening and sticky. It amazed me to think I'd taken something so enormous.

Back in England I obtained my own version of that monster and I use it when Roger fails to satisfy me, always getting satisfaction. I wish someone like Georgie was here to apply it to me. That would really be the ideal situation. Any offers?

Gwen, Godalming

Late-Night Shopping

I would like to share an experience with you that happened to me recently, after a successful contact from a contact magazine. I took part in some interesting swapping with my then girlfriend in the early 1980's, before meeting my ex-wife. After the breakup of my marriage last year, I decided to meet some couples as an extra man.

I arranged to meet this couple, Denise and Eric at a pub some distance from both our houses. When I entered the bar I noticed them straight away. Denise, who was a real exhibitionist, was attracting all sorts of looks from the male customers. She was in her late thirties but still had a stunning figure, most of which she was showing off. She had on the classic short white skirt and a tiny leopard skin top, although you could see she still wore a bra. Eric was both loving and hating every minute, smiling but still squirming slightly. He was obviously pleased to recognise me from my photos. I got a drink and went over to join them.

Denise greeted me with a hug as if we were long-lost friends. The lads at the bar looked a little disappointed, but Eric was beaming. He wanted to leave fast, anxious to get down to the next stage, but Denise wanted to stay, milking in the admiration from me and the lads at the bar. We got up to leave shortly afterwards and I followed them to their house in my car.

I don't know what happened in their car, but when we

got back to their house, Denise appeared to have gone off the whole idea. Eric tried to talk her round, but I think that she was having cold feet. I couldn't help feeling that Eric was keener on the watching than Denise was on sex. Whilst Eric was out of the room, she confessed to me that although she got a real thrill in the pub, it was the exhibitionism that turned her on. It wasn't me, in fact she really fancied me, it was just she couldn't have sex in front of Eric and he was determined to watch.

It got me thinking of a game I used to play with my swapping girlfriend. I explained it to Denise and Eric and they agreed to try it the following week. The game involved me and Denise going shopping with Eric being just an onlooker from afar. I would choose revealing outfits for Denise to try on, which she would model for me (and Eric) in the shop. Hopefully it would turn her on enough to finish off this time.

We met for a late-night shopping evening. Denise, as asked, dressed quite soberly, but I knew she would be going home in something completely different. We went from shop to shop trying on outfits. Each time the skirt was a little shorter, the top a little more see-through. Denise was in her element and it wasn't long before I pursuaded her to remove her bra. She came out of the changing room and gave it to me. I slipped it to Eric while Denise was changing back. His face was a picture; I thought he was going to burst a blood vessel.

Soon after that, I picked out the clothes that Denise was going to wear home. One of the sports shops was having a sale of tennis clothes and there was one little dress that was going to drive everyone wild. It was button-through with a scooped neck and a tiny ra-ra skirt. With a t-shirt and knickers it was still fairly racy but, without them, was positively indecent. Denise was now flushing heavily, but agreed to wear it, no t-shirt or bra but still with matching frilly knickers. She got changed and put her other clothes in a bag, which I gave to Eric. While he put them in the car, I explained the trick to Denise that we were going to play on Eric. She would try on a bikini and we would convince the assistant to allow me into the changing room to look whilst Eric, of course, would be trapped outside, not sure what was happening.

She agreed at once and, with Eric in tow, we went straight to the chemists to loudly buy some condoms. Before Eric could stop us, we had swopped shops, chosen our bikini and were in the changing rooms. His face was a picture as we went inside, giggling to each other. What was supposed to happen, was that I would masturbate into one of the condoms and Denise would give it, tied up, to Eric. I was unprepared for what happened next.

As soon as the door closed, Denise grabbed my head in both hands and started to kiss me passionately. Whether it was the fact that Eric couldn't see us or her inhibitions had gone, I will never know but she was like a wild animal. Not caring that they could obviously hear outside, she unzipped my fly and pulled out my tool. After all the sexual build-up not surprisingly it was rock hard. In fact I had had trouble hiding it for the last half hour. Ripping the condom packet from me, she rolled one on. I eased her knickers down, God was she wet. The secretions had soaked the gusset of the tennis panties. As soon as they were off she wrapped her legs around mine. 'For God's sake, fuck me' she whispered. 'I've been dying for this ever since I put this dress on. I feel like a whore in it, just make me come'.

There was no way I was going to last for long and I

shot my load in what seemed like seconds and I suppose was. I don't even know if Denise came but she certainly took charge. Slipping the condom from me, she wrapped it in her knickers. 'Come on', she said and walked out with me in tow. She handed the package to Eric, saying, 'We're going for a coffee, leave us alone'. As we left the store she wrapped her arm around me and headed for the escalator.

Obviously she couldn't care now, the tiny skirt was flapping from side to side showing glimpses of her bare ass and cunt. As we got on the glass-sided escalator she lifted one leg onto the step above. I'm sure half the males in the shopping centre saw her dripping pussy as we went up. She wouldn't give Eric a chance to interfere as she grabbed me closely. We took up two raised stools at her insistence. We were surrounded at a reasonable distance by about ten or twelve single guys, all staring as she rubbed my thigh between her legs.

Eric could not take any more. I was already hard again. I couldn't imagine how he was coping, having watched us for over an hour. He quickly left for the Gents, to wank himself off for sure. As soon as he left, so did we, almost running for my car. As soon as we got inside, Denise slipped a finger into her cunt and placed another on her clit. 'Find a place to fuck,' she shouted, 'I need a prick inside me. If it's not yours, I'll find someone else'.

It was a strange feeling, driving furiously around trying to find a secluded spot, whilst Denise rubbed herself to orgasm after orgasm on the seat beside me. I don't know if anyone saw her, but it would have made their day if they did. As soon as we stopped, she stuffed my prick in her mouth. I certainly didn't need that, I was close to coming again. I pulled it out, rolled on a condom, lowered the seat and fucked her for all I was worth. We finished my packet of three soon afterwards. I had to go into a pub to get some more. Denise was past the point of caring now as she followed me in, hair dishevelled and half her buttons undone. Thank God there was no-one in the gents. Denise wanted to have me in there, but I managed to get her back in the car without any fuss.

Poor Eric, he looked like death when we got back to their house. Denise was a picture, with come in her hair and all the buttons on her dress ripped off. I was too tired to care as he hustled her inside and slammed the door on me. I never saw them again. Eric slammed down the phone when I rang and I didn't want to push it. After all, I had had the experience of a lifetime and anything else would have been pale by comparison.

Simon, Exeter

On the Menu

'I swear you've got the tastiest cunt I've ever eaten,' my boss told me from between my thighs. He was the owner and sole chef of the little café where I part-timed as a waitress and washer-up. At that moment I was perched on the edge of the kitchen sink with my knees raised and shoes planted on his shoulders while he was busily tonguing my pussy. Not for the first time, during visits to the kitchen, he was making me come by sucking and licking my sex.

No doubt there are those who'd say that was blatent sexual harassment, an abuse of his power as my employer. Certainly Harry would have ended up before a tribunal if he'd tried on with others what he did with me. From the first day he'd given my tits a feel, fondled my bum in passing, asked me how often and how well my husband fucked me, and generally made a pest of himself – unless you were the kind that agreed a little hanky-panky helped to pass the working day.

Harry's wife was a frigid bitch, the kind of ice maiden who would drive any husband to seek something elsewhere. She sat unmoving behind the till, taking the payments as our customers left. Although the real boss of the café, she insisted on her share of the tips I was left as waitress. She complained if she thought I was slow in serving on the few times we were really busy and was generally a pain in the arse. So, going back into the café, glowing from being made to come on her husband's tongue, added to the pleasure I'd been given in the kitchen.

I'd stopped wearing knickers, sure that Harry would corner me and want to 'go downstairs for lunch' as he liked to call it. Luckily for him, and me too, it was something I'd always loved since being a bridesmaid at my sister's wedding. At sixteen and drunk for the first time, I had had multiple orgasms from the best man licking me out on the back seat of the bus that had brought a party of guests. We were parked in the hotel's car park and when I got there I found the other bridesmaid (my sister) being fucked by the lad who is now my husband. Told how big and good he was by my sister, when he asked me for a date later, I was glad to say I'd see him.

He was good at fucking me too, though surprisingly not very experienced in varying positions and oral sex, which by the time we married I'd sampled with boys at home and on Spanish holidays. I taught my hubby to vary, to take me dog-fashion or let me ride over him, which I admit he took to with gusto. Same as when I told him one night that I'd waited long enough. I'd been sucking him off and wanted him to reciprocate. 'Lick me out, eat me,' I told him, and he couldn't get enough of it after that.

When on early shift, he'd bring me up tea and toast in bed, then kiss me goodbye. This was by drawing aside the duvet and lowering his mouth on my twat as I parted my legs. The usual genital kiss went on until I was moaning and coming. Licking out became such a certain climax-maker for me that, when I started work in Harry's café and he was begging for a fuck, I agreed he could have a 'muff-diving' session, if he was into that.

'My favourite thing,' he said, hoisting me up on the draining board, removing my knickers, and kissing my cunt lips. He teased me with little flicks of his tongue around my clitty until I was groaning and pleading with him to lick me out. Harry was no slouch. He took his time even with his fearsome missis just yards away. Of course he knew that she would not desert her seat at the till as long as diners were there who might nip off without paying. To me, it added to the thrill that at any moment she might just possibly come through and catch us. In the meantime Harry's mouth and lips, expertly applied, made me wetter as his long tongue snaked into my pussy and sucked enticingly on my clit.

That first time I seemed to explode on his tongue. I felt his hand clamp over my mouth as I began to shout out my pleasure. As I finished work later, I put my hand in my coat pocket and counted two fivers among the change of my amount of tips. That thrilled me too, to think I'd been paid for enjoying myself. It was some weeks later that Harry said that some of his male customers fancied me. I knew them, of course, because I served them. A night or two later I went home from work with one I fancied myself. Parked on wasteland, along the back seat of his car, I was thoroughly licked out and paid for the pleasure.

I was waitressing for money, having a large mortgage to meet every month, and with Harry putting me in the way of clients who'd pay to go down on me, this suited me nicely. I enjoyed my extra comes and the money was helpful. Of course, my clients wanted to fuck me as well but again I stuck to oral only. Except for the man I really fancied, and he was only allowed a fuck if wearing a condom. My husband hasn't a clue of any of this going on, of course, but what he doesn't know won't kill him. Harry says I'm the best item on his menu, heartily recommended.

Alison, Scarborough

Like Mother, Like Daughter

My wife Jean and I were both on the second time around. My first had ended in divorce, when my then wife had caught me bare-arsed screwing her mother doggie-fashion in our lounge while a porno video was running on the telly. Teresa, my first wife, was dead against porn and never allowed it in the house, the prudish bitch. I think the fact I'd defied her and brought a blue video into her home infuriated her as much as catching me shafting her mum.

Perhaps more, in fact, for Teresa and her mother had not been on speaking terms for a long time. Two more different women you couldn't find: the mother being jolly and game for anything while her daughter's joy in life was polishing and dusting her palace. Sex was a no-no with Teresa unless I'd been good, like buying her the latest vacuum cleaner or some other handy-dandy household appliance. For my reward I might just be allowed a fuck, which would have been great if I were into necrophilia. Teresa would lie below me, cold and lifeless, her nightie raised just enough to allow access to her minge.

So unused was her sex that I expected to find it had healed up. When Harriet, her mother, sympathised with me, stating that as a widow good nookie was what she missed most, I offered my services. She was plump and shapely, with that smooth white skin that doesn't tan, as is usual for a redhead. Twice a week at least we'd meet after that and almost had a race to see who could strip first. Once I was naked, I'd be ordered to go down on her. When I fucked the tight cleavage of her fat tits, she'd urge me to gush all over her. Available for spanking, wanking and fucking, she brightened my life no end while I suffered her daughter.

So chuffed was I with Harriet's uninhibited desires, I boasted about our romps to a mate. He was intrigued, with the result that he sought out Harriet, courted her and married her. That taught me to keep my big mouth shut. Finally divorced from Teresa, but without her ma to console me, then I met Jean and found what I'd been looking for, a woman as randy for cock as one could want. She'd fucked her first husband into a shadow, she told me, and warned me I'd be the same.

After a year or so of marriage I was still holding out, giving as good as I got. Then Jean's daughter, Trish, came to visit from Australia where she had emigrated to work as a nurse and married an Aussie. Leaving him behind, she came to be bridesmaid at a school chum's wedding. Trish was twenty-four, well-built like her mum, and with a few drinks in her at the wedding reception, insisted that her 'new dad' as she teasingly called me, gave her a dance. Right away as we took to the floor in a slow smoochy dance, her arms went around my neck.

'How are you doing with that mum of mine?' she said wickedly, pressing her ample tits into my chest. 'Are you getting plenty?'

'Plenty of what?' I asked, as if I didn't know.

'Plenty of this,' the horny bitch laughed, tilting her pelvis and rubbing her cunt mound against my crotch. I could have put the talk down to drink, but knew she was a game girl like her mother. To keep in the spirit of the thing, as she pressed her boobs into my chest and ground her crotch against mine, I warned her that if there was any more of that as her new dad, I'd be forced to put her across my knee. 'Ooh, promises, promises,' the naughty creature giggled. 'On my bare bottom? I can hardly wait.'

The following afternoon was a scorcher. My wife, a doctor's receptionist, was working. I'm a self-employed electrician. So I finished one job and called it a day. On my return, I showered, walking back into the bedroom drying myself and glancing idly out of the window into our garden. Sheltered by tall trees and hedges, there on the lawn below I saw my gorgeous step-daughter sunning herself in the absolute buff. I admired the curve of her buttocks as she lay face down, then admired her firm tits as she rolled over and got up to enter the house.

As she entered the kitchen she must have spotted my tool-bag, calling out my name. I shouted back I was upstairs, my guts surging with arousal, wondering if I'd turn down the chance to fuck her if offered and knowing I wouldn't. I wrapped the bath towel around me as she entered the bedroom with not a stitch covering her curvaceous body. She stood there flashing her big tits and plump hairy minge, her eyes going to the bulge under my towel as my cock grew bigger. 'Let me see it. Drop the towel,' she said. 'You want to, don't you?'

As I let the towel fall to the floor she advanced towards me. Heart pounding, my prick leapt bolt upright and she reached out to clasp it in her hand. 'I want it,' she said, her voice still steady and calm, the cool bitch. 'I've been without it too long for me. I'm fed up wanking myself. Would you mind fucking me? Mother's on the evening shift, isn't she? We've plenty of time.'

'You don't mind being screwed by your stepfather?' I asked, my eyes on her gorgeous tits and the dark triangle of hair and pouting lips of her quim. 'You'd do that to your mum?'

'What she won't know won't hurt her,' Trish said. Her tits were right in front of my face so I cupped them and began kissing them, sucking on each nipple in turn as she stroked my dong. It takes a strong man to refuse a amply-built naked girl who is massaging your dick and says she wants fucked. I guided her to the bed and lowered her across it. As she spread her legs I went in face first with my tongue extended. I traced my tongue around the outer lips, inserted the tip inside and tasted the pungent juice of her arousal.

'Yes! Tongue fuck me, you randy sod!' I heard her exclaim, the calmness in her voice replaced by urgency. My head was grabbed, forced between her thighs as my tongue probed. As her back arched and her pelvis jerked, I knew she'd already had a strong come, climaxing against my face. 'Now fuck me! Use your prick to make me come again!' she cried out. Moving up, I found her thighs widely parted, her hand directing my prick to her cleft. 'Fuck me properly, don't you dare come until I want you to,' I was told. 'Shove it all up!'

'I'll show you how it's done,' I told her in return, fully sheathed and bringing her back to the boil as her hips thrust. She screamed 'Keep it in!' as I withdrew, stroked her clitty with the bulbous knob before sensuously sliding it into her again. Her groan and a long drawn-out breath showed I'd taken her to the brink again, her spasms increasing until she was out of control. A further climax shook as I had her deeply penetrated. Then I rolled over with her on top of me without 'uncunting', as they say. I urged her to work her arse on my throbbing stalk.

Happy to lie back and watch the expression on her

contorted face, I let her dictate the pace as she bucked, squirmed and ground her cunt against my rampant dick. Her lovely tits danced tantalisingly over my mouth as I craned my neck to catch her nipples in my lips. As I felt her pace increasing and knew she was about to come again, I allowed myself to lose control. Jet after jet of delayed hot spunk was spurted deep into her crevice. It was hardly the time to enquire whether she was on the pill or not and, not caring at the moment of firing, I did wonder if I'd impregnated her.

Too late was the cry, anyway, as she kissed and hugged me for giving her such relief. 'Mum has kept on about what a good shagger you are,' Trish said to me on regaining her breath. 'A right horny bugger, she said you were. I just had to find out for myself.' We got up and showered, removing all the sweat of our lustful exertions before her mother returned. For the next two weeks of her stay with us, the romp was repeated regularly. As a self-employed bloke, I'm afraid a few customers had to wait for my services.

Roy, Lancs

Pregnant Pause

My husband was never mad about making love. If I waited for him to make an approach weeks would pass and I'd be forced to make all the running myself. To satisfy myself I took myself in hand and gave myself a good relieving come at least twice a week. I wanted a baby so gave up the pill and, after some months of trying, at last conceived. Robert became afraid to touch me after that, treating me as if I was fragile when in fact I'd never felt in such robust health.

At six months pregnant, I found my sex drive was keener than ever. Robert meanwhile, seemed to have gone off me completely. Scared of rolling on me or bumping my swollen belly in the night, he even moved into the spare bedroom. When I complained of this to his mother, she said she'd advised him to do it! I should have known, asking an old fuddy-duddy like her, and didn't wonder about how her son had turned out as prudish as she.

I didn't think being preggy made me unattractive, for I thought there was something sexy about me when I looked at myself in the mirror. My breasts had become udders, real teats, fat and bloated with the nipples thrusting out like thimbles. My tum curved out and down like the side of the moon, so full it made my cunt and fuzz of hair disappear out of sight between my thighs. When the local midwife popped in during the usual pre-natal visits, she said I was remarkably well.

She was perhaps forty, plump and matronly with a

sweet face. We'd always chatted during her calls and therefore I told her I was fine but my sex drive was stronger than ever. What's wrong with that? she said, explaining that many women find the hormone changes during pregnancy greatly increase their sex needs. She laughed and patted my tummy, saying what was in there wouldn't be harmed by normal intercourse. 'So you've straightened me out about that,' I told her jokingly. 'Now straighten out my husband. He thinks I'm strictly a no-go area. Meanwhile I'm bursting for a good fuck, or a climax of any kind at least. I haven't tried lately, the shape I'm in, but I suppose masturbation is allowable in my case?'

The way she looked at me made me wonder if she'd taken offence. Her face seemed contorted, her speech thick and unsure as she answered. 'There's no need to feel deprived,' she said. 'It's not good for you in your state. You must be relaxed and kept satisfied. Oral sex could be a wonderful way of giving you strong climaxes. It's harmless, quite hygienic if you wash your vagina, as I know you do. The medical term is cunnilingus and I guarantee you'd find it both thrilling and satisfying.

'I'm sure I would,' I said drily, 'but my husband already refuses to lick me out or tongue me. I've asked him. I'd like it. So that's not on, although thank you for suggesting it.'

'I'd do it for you,' my midwife friend said suddenly. 'It would not be the first time I've done it to another woman. Haven't you guessed that I'm gay? I'd like to do it, for my own kind of pleasure as well as for yours.'

'I–I don't think so,' I said, hoping that she would not be too offended. But after she'd gone, thinking about it, I wondered if I'd been too hasty. She was a nice, cuddly person, and no doubt a good and experienced licker-out of cunts. She'd probably been a lesbian since her teen years, as true ones are, never marrying. I pictured her face burrowing between my thighs and her tongue ploughing my furrow, lapping up the juices and her lips closing over my clitty giving it deliciously arousing sucks. The thought made be feel quite faint and horny. I *knew* I should have accepted her offer.

It was still on my mind the following morning, and thinking about it had made me hornier than ever. I bathed, put on my nightie and went back to lie on my bed. I phoned her mobile number. She was in her car, sounding delighted to hear from me.

'About what you suggested yesterday,' I began. 'I–I want you to you-know-what.' She arrived some twenty minutes later, during which time I'd had second thoughts but did not want to offend her again. I waited nervously until she let herself in and came upstairs. I noticed she wore a simple print dress instead of her midwife's uniform. 'What a pretty nightie,' she complimented me, 'and panties to match. Take off your nightie, my dear, let me see you.' I did so, excited by displaying myself. I had decided that I would do whatever she asked.

Unlike the men I've known, apart from my husband, seeing me with only brief panties on did not inspire her to leap at me. Instead she took long moments to regard me admiringly, making me feel beautiful and wanted. I'd heard that women making love to each other were unhurried and gentle, now I knew why women sometimes preferred their own sex. 'Your breasts are beautiful,' she whispered. 'So full and firm. I want you to touch them, hold them like you'd want somebody else to hold them.'

Instantly my hands went up to cup and fondle my

breasts. I sighed at the pleasure of my own touch, realising that doing it while being watched added to the erotic mood building within me. 'Does that feel nice?' she enquired. I nodded but said, 'Not as nice as if you were touching them.' She smiled and moved my hands, replacing them with her own, gently cupping the swollen undersides of my breasts. 'I'd like your mouth on them,' I said meekly. 'On my nipples. Suck them, please.' It seemed my nipples jutted out proudly for her to suck. She drew each one into her mouth, arousing me further before she stopped.

'Anywhere else you'd like me to suck?' she asked teasingly, knowing she had me where she wanted, and in truth where I wanted to be. I nodded and she eased down my briefs, casting them aside. 'Open your legs for me,' she ordered. A finger slipping into my moist vagina made me squirm in pleasure. 'You're warm and wet, you naughty thing,' she said. 'Just ready for the tongue, my dear.' Her head was between my thighs, leaning forward so that the tip of her tongue brushed my outer sex-lips. 'Oh yes.' I heard myself moan. 'Put it in me.'

Probing deeply, she began to swirl her stiffened tongue in sinuous circles, using the base of her chin to increase the pressure of her tongue against my vaginal walls. Going into me ardently, I could feel her forehead resting on the down-curve of my curving belly as she tongued and lapped. Soon she had me going berserk with pleasure. I fell back on the bed, tipping up my pelvis and allowing her greater access. Her pointed tongue finally settled on the bud of my clitty, followed by her lips enclosing about its little dome, sucking until I was screaming, jerking about and going into repeated climaxes.

On each visit, my obliging midwife gave me relief

with her tongue, almost up to the day of the birth of my daughter, by which time I lay face down and bottom up as the most comfortable way to be served. Robert and I are still together, he's a nice man and a good father, but nowadays I have lovers of both sexes to keep me satisfied.

Margaret B., Lothians

Blowing the Whistle

I was desperate to tell my best friend's husband that she was having affairs with other guys. My friend is twenty-eight and married to what I consider the perfect man. They have three great kids and a fabulous house. He gives her everything she wants and is a wonderful father. As a single girl, he is just what I dream of in a husband.

So I was niggled that she was having affairs, both with men and women. She admitted to me that she felt guilty sometimes, but such is her sex drive that she does it again and again. She accused me of being jealous, and reminded me that we'd once had fling while working as air hostesses. On a stopover in a hotel she had come to my bedroom and made love to me, with kisses all over our naked bodies and oral sex as well.

This had led to us always sharing a room on overseas flights. The fact that we were sleeping together was common knowledge among the flight crew. Once, while at an overnight stop, it was my birthday and to my shame I was presented with a large vibrating dildo. That night my friend Janet used it on me and I on her, bringing us to multiple climaxes. Neither of us were true lesbians however and Janet still had her pick of men.

Her husband had no idea of what was going on. I told her she didn't know when she was well off. She laughed and said it sounds like you would like him for yourself. So I called on him, being invited in and wondering why he didn't seem surprised to see me.

Shown into the living room, I paused while wondering how to start telling him that his wife slept around. He took my arm and led me upstairs. I was too startled to ask what was he doing.

'You should have told Janet before that you were into threesomes, Denise,' he said. 'When I was told you were coming today, I said none better to make up a trio.' Still lost for words, I was guided into a bedroom where Janet lay back on the coverlet, stark naked. In her hand she held the vibrator we had used together, smiling knowingly as if daring me to say anything about her affairs with others.

Both she and her husband began undressing me, their hands fondling my intimate places, their kisses hot on my face, breasts and cunt. In a tangle of arms and legs, the three of us fell across the bed, both Janet and her husband positioning me between them, their hands and mouths used in the lewdest fashion to subdue me. In turn my nipples and vagina were sucked, my will reduced as I began to respond.

I welcomed Janet's husband as he mounted me, accepting his rigid length wantonly and urging him to satisfy me. Even as he was plunging into me, his wife crouched over my face and lowered her sex onto my mouth. It was impossible to remain unaffected and it was hours later before I left their house. As Janet saw me to the door she asked me what my fiancé would think if informed of that afternoon's orgy.

The implication was 'Keep my secret and I'll keep yours'. 'Do call again, Denise,' she said smugly, adding that given the chance I was as bad as she was. But she wasn't as clever as she thought for I came back another day when I knew she was out and now her gorgeous husband is fucking me behind her back. So I suppose we're all quits.

Denise, Poole

4. All I Really, Really Want

Girl Power
Tits Out for the Lads
Whatever Moira Wants
Doing the Double
Bedtime Stories
The Best Chest
Victim of Love
The Sweet Taste of Success
Sauce for the Goose
Just Good Neighbours
Collecting the Rent
Among Our Souvenirs

Girl Power

To cheer me up because my fiancé had turned out be a louse, a schoolfriend took me out for the evening. We called in at an all-girl bar, lesbian of course, and at once I was 'pulled' by a tall woman dressed in black. Her bleached white hair was cropped short and she wore heavy eye shadow. On seeing me, and saying later I looked like a shy little virgin, she pursed her pouty lips at me and made kissing sounds.

Helen was so obviously the butch-dyke type of gay woman that my friend began to laugh. Not for long, however, for she was silenced with an icy glare that scared us both stiff. The woman took my arm and led me docilely to the handkerchief-sized dance floor. '*You* are with *me* tonight, my sweet,' I was told sternly, and I nodded. Never before had I been attracted to women or even thought about it, yet I found this dominant woman irresistible.

A moment later I was clasped tight in her arms, dancing to slow smoochy music with her marble-firm breasts and pointy nipples digging into my breasts. Below, I felt her hard pubic bone pressed against my mound. A deliberate slow grinding movement began as she gyrated her pelvis in sexual motions, crotch to crotch like a man fucking. It became obvious to the women around us what she was doing to make me aroused. She kissed me full on the mouth with probing tongue and from the smirks of the lesbians around they knew Helen was seducing me.

'Are you still living at home with mummy?' she asked snidely, When I told her I was at college and had my own flat, she was even more scornful. 'You could pass for a fourteen-year-old and a pretty naive one at that. Don't tell me you're still a virgin?' When I said with a tremble in my voice, fearing the power she already had over me, that whether or not I was still a virgin was none of her business and I wouldn't tell her, she pulled me even closer to her and leered into my face.

'You'll tell me all I want to know,' she said with menace. 'If you want to be my little girl, then you'll have no secrets. Even if I have to spank and whip them out of you,' she added, making me shiver. Yet I was thrilled at the thought. My friend was getting worried watching us. She came up and nervously suggested that it was time for us to go home.

'You go,' Helen said forcibly. 'Simone is staying with me. She's coming home with me tonight. Isn't that right, lover?' I found myself nodding as I indicated to my best friend that I was going off with this lesbian stranger.

Once in the taxi to Helen's flat, she fondled my breasts and pressed long lewd kisses on my mouth which left me breathless and aroused. 'Have you ever had another woman fuck you with a dildo, girl?' she whispered between the torrid kisses. When I shook my head shyly, she hugged me and said she had so much to show me.

We undressed facing each other in her bedroom. I felt strange to be doing so for another woman but trembled with excitement. She praised my breasts, pressed kisses on the nipples, ran her fingers over my aroused and moist vulva before slipping her fingers inside me. I lay spread out on the bed with my legs in the air while she fingered and licked my vagina at the same time until I was squawking and coming frantically, shamelessly crying out for her to use me as she wished.

We ended up in bed with Helen strapped into a monstrous dildo. She mounted me like a man, fucking me to more shattering orgasms. In the morning, after a night spent in uninhibited lesbian lust, I was rather shocked by my lewdness and other indiscretions. I had put my face between her legs as ordered and lapped up her juices, tonguing her repeatedly to orgasm. I'd been over her knee for a spanking when once I dared suggest it was time for me to go home. I was left in no doubt who was my mistress – and that was how I wanted it.

With Helen as my lover, I was introduced to lesbian groups who shared our way of life. I felt men could not compete in giving me the thrills and sexual satisfaction I got from other women. I was taken to the most uninhibited parties, all of us girls and women naked and indulging in the most lewd fun and games without a blush or shame. It all seemed so natural to us. I'm sure other women are unaware of what they are missing.

Helen allowed me certain latitude with other women, while always keeping an eye on me to make sure I remembered I was hers. Any show of fancying other girls during our parties meant severe punishment on return to the flat we shared. A strapping while bent over was a painful reminder that I must remember my place. It also left me very aroused and I would plead shamelessly to be given a climax. In time, of course, Helen and I went our own way, but I kept up with the lesbian scene, having several lovers before settling for my present girlfriend.

Of course bitchiness and petty jealousies are as prevalent as in male and female affairs. I have witnessed women coming to blows over the favours of another girl.

But meetings can be purely for sexual pleasure. Most of us shave our pubic hair, for genital kisses and tonguing are far nicer on bare sexual regions. Spanking each other is fun, using either our palms, canes or leather straps. The hardness of the punishment is left to the one on the receiving end. Battery-operated vibrators and strap-on dildoes are used, often by a couple who provide entertainment for the watchers gathered around.

My latest partner, Gillian, reminds me of myself when younger. At her first lesbian get-together, I 'pulled' her as Helen had once pulled me. She was an innocent, vulnerable to seduction. We slept together and, being a big strapping girl, she soon took the dominant role in our relationship. I'm sure there are multitudes of secret lesbians, married women who would like a fling with a female but who dare not try it out.

A lesbian friend who is a masseuse in a health centre for women reckons her clients come to her for one reason only, to have the thrill of exposing their bodies to another woman and be fondled sexually by feminine hands. She is often begged to bring 'relief' to the woman on the massage table. These clients do not like to own up to their lesbian tendencies but, believe me, they have nothing to be ashamed of.

Simone, Middlesex

Tits Out for The Lads

During the early years of our marriage I was extremely jealous and possessive, uneasy if Joyce even spoke to another man. As the years passed I mellowed. It seemed that Joyce had no interest in other men or in having sex, apart from our usual Saturday night fuck with the lights out. It just shows we should never take anyone for granted!

After the kids left home and the prospect of our usual South Coast holiday seemed as dreary and boring as our marriage, I suggested we try abroad for a change. I plumped for Spain, hopeful of topless beaches, but when a friend offered the use of his house near a beach in Cyprus, I felt it too good a chance to refuse. At forty-two Joyce had a good figure, so once in Cyprus and seeing others on the beach in bikinis, she surprised me by buying one. I saw men look at her. She was quite busty up top and rounded below, and I remembered how jealous I'd been years before.

One night she asked if we could go dancing at the local bar, which was another surprise. I was also surprised at the number of men who came to our table and asked her to dance. Her fuller figure certainly attracted men. One young chap had several dances with her. He joined us at our table and told us he was a soldier stationed nearby. We found he was a Geordie like ourselves and agreed to meet him on the beach next morning.

During the evening it became obvious to me that the

young guy had the hots for my wife and that Joyce enjoyed his attention. The lights at the tables around the square of dancing space were turned down low. I excused myself to go to the toilet and, on making my way back to our table, saw Joyce and the young soldier kissing. I thought that he couldn't be much older than eighteen, then remembered that I'd read that men reached their sexual peak around that age. I don't know what made me do it, but I stood back and watched as she returned his kisses.

I saw him fondle her breasts outside her dress, and what her hand was doing under the table I could only guess. Watching them gave me a tremendous thrill as well as a terrific hard-on. For some time I'd been fantasising about watching my wife having sex with another man and this was no doubt why I'd found the spectacle so arousing. When I rejoined them I said nothing of what I'd seen.

When I got Joyce home I saw her slip into bed without her nightie and was excited to think that the lad had got her worked up enough to want to fuck. As I joined her in bed she pressed her bare breasts to my chest and threw a leg across me, whispering that she wanted a fuck. I joked, while stroking her cunt lips and pressing my hugely stiff dick against her leg, that she'd been turned on by the young bloke's obvious letch for her. The way she giggled, showed she liked the thought. 'That's very well, my love,' I said, 'but what if he wants to take you to bed and fuck you?' The very idea sent us both wild with lust. She dragged me across her and I thrust deep into her cunt, fucking her like never before.

On the beach next day we found Brian, the young squaddie, with three of his mates. One was another white lad and the other two were strapping black youths. They all made a fuss of Joyce and teased her about wearing her bikini top as others around were topless. Then they splashed about in the sea. Watching her acting like a teenager had me in two minds. On the one hand, she deserved to let her hair down. On the other, things were obviously getting out of hand. When Joyce invited the lads back to our holiday house for coffee and sandwiches, I feared the worst. To fantasise about your wife being fucked by other men is one thing; seeing it actually happen is another. Yet I didn't speak out.

At least she hadn't taken off her bikini top, I thought to myself. But once in the house and not on a crowded beach, and encouraged by them flattering her – 'come on, we want to see those gorgeous tits,' one told her – she threw aside the bra, wobbling her big firm boobs at the boys. They cried out *MORE* and she turned to waggle her bottom at them and then lowered her briefs. Stepping out of them she turned to show herself full frontal, with firm big teats and a prominently bulging cunt mound festooned with bushy hair.

The young soldiers gathered around her, too far gone to be stopped by me. They began to kiss her. She had a mouth on each nipple, one on her cunt and one boy kneeling behind her, tonguing her bottom. Then she was hoisted up and carried off to the bedroom, her protests merely token. 'The bitch loves it, loves those boys making free with her,' I growled to myself, standing in the open bedroom door, unable to tear myself away from the sight. The boys stripped quickly, all of them athletic and with fiercely erect tools. What I was to witness over the next seven hours was my wife being shagged senseless by four lusty young men.

They fucked her in every possible position and did with her all that can be sexually achieved with a willing woman. I saw her shafted front, back and sideways. Fucked on hands and knees while her mouth was filled with cock at the other end. Never have I heard such lewd vocal accompaniments to the orgy, my wife as loud and crude as the young men as they penetrated her from every angle. 'Get in there, knob!' I heard one of the black youths yell as he thrust with my wife's legs over his shoulders. 'Fuck it all up me! Fill me, split me, pile-drive me!' Joyce screamed as yet another lad's arse was jerking in a frenzy as he screwed her. 'Don't come, leave it up my cunt!' was another plea that issued from her mouth and, most surprising of all when being fucked to yet another climax, was to hear her beg '*Yesss*, fill me up, shoot your thick juice up me and give me a baby.' I was just thankful that she was sterilised. Otherwise I'm sure enough come was pumped into her greedy cunt to make a kid of one colour or another.

The boys showed what they thought of her as they shafted her, got a tit-ride and were sucked off by shouting 'Take this in your mouth, you slut,' and 'How d'you like a big black cock up your fanny, you horny cow?' Far from being offended, she urged them to continue, thrilled to be called bitch, slut and cocksucker in the throes of being brought off.

The boys had guard duty or whatever that night, otherwise I'm sure they'd have been there until morning. When they left they told me what a great sport my wife was, and a terrific fuck as well. Brian said she was the kind of woman he hoped to have as a wife, saying I was a lucky guy. Joyce was left fucked out on the bed, glistening with body sweat from her exertions, her cunt swollen and pouting from use. The mixed juices of their glutinous emissions cloyed her hair and tits, while more of it leaked from every one of her orifices.

In time she stretched out languidly and murmured she'd never felt so sated and sexually fulfilled. It must be every woman's fantasy, she said, adding that it was hers. And I'd never thought she was the type. She thanked me for letting her live out her dream. Then I helped her to the shower. 'What a pity you didn't take pictures of all that,' she said later. I'd thought of it but where would I have got such prints developed? We both agreed the boys would come back for more 'now they'd been up there' as Joyce put it cheekily. No doubt about it, she loved being the plaything of four lusty boys.

So I bought a Polaroid camera, determined to have a momento of the next session. Even better, they brought a camcorder so I've got my Joyce being shagged in all positions in instant colour photos and on videotapes, which the lads presented to us. Now we are back home, if I see my wife looking wistful, I imagine she's thinking of the orgies in Cyprus. We've been offered the same house next year and no doubt she'll be entertaining some more brave lads in the way she knows best.

Ted and Joyce, Newcastle

Whatever Moira Wants

Edward made no secret of the fact that he fancied my wife. And if the way Moira flirted and danced close to him was any pointer, it was plain she fancied him. Trouble was that she'd found me fucking a neighbour in our marital bed. When she popped home in her lunch hour to pick up her credit card she'd heard the sounds of shagging. Moira had that little lapse to hold over me.

Our neighbour Alice was on her knees, tilted and back dipped, gripping the wooden headboard for dear life as I pounded into her. Hardly the time for one's wife to walk in. After that you can say our marriage definitely cooled. Moira moved me into the spare room, and she began to say how Edward complimented her at work, saying how attractive she was, how well she dressed. 'How well you'd look undressed, he means,' I told her snidely. 'He's a right sleazy character and only wants to get in your knickers.'

'He's young, good-looking and successful,' she countered, taking pleasure in reminding me that Alice, whom I'd been caught fucking, was a middle-aged housewife. At a time when we were getting back to normal life and I was expecting to be welcomed back into Moira's bed, she came home late from work one night flushed and distressed. She sat on my knee and began to sob. 'I don't know what to do,' she moaned. 'I want Edward but I don't want to leave you. He— he's been fucking me—'

'How could you, you bitch,' I said, but she threw at me that I was as bad, fucking Alice from next door and how long had that been going on? I could have told her for several years, since Alice told me (and I took the hint) that her hubby George had given up making love to her. Pleasantly plump and excitingly big-titted, there were many good fucks to be had with Alice. There still was during my time in the doghouse with Moira, which had made sleeping in the spare room not such a punishment. However, I swore to my wife that it had been a one-off. 'Bet your fuck wasn't the first with that big bastard Edward,' I accused, and she agreed!

She confessed all the details, almost as if she were proud of having an affair. Working late, she told me, one thing had led to another and they'd fucked across the desk in his office. I groaned when she recalled she'd been made to come several times. Listening to her detailing subsequent fucks: in his car, a friend's flat, in *our* bed when I'd been away, was torture as well as helplessly arousing. Her position on my lap meant my dong had been pressed against her cushiony arse cheeks. Hearing how Edward fucked her, sucked her, and did all kinds of lewd things to her breasts and fanny, made my cock rise in sympathy.

It stiffened and stretched, a tight cylinder of flesh that she made sure fitted snugly into the crease of her arse cheeks by subtly shifting her position. She was excited and knew that I was too. When I insisted she give me all the lurid details she did not spare a word.

It seemed Edward was a deal more imaginative than me. He had, for instance, ordered her to strip and go bare-ass across his knee for a spanking. She'd jacked him off with her silk knickers. She'd sucked him off in his car in the firm's car park. We both got so worked up talking about it that I lowered her to the carpet and told her I was going to fuck the arse off her. She let me, and it was a memorable screw, the pair of us going at it like sex maniacs. It struck me that hearing about my wife having it off with another bloke had given us the best sex ever.

I knew by the flushed and bright-eyed way Moira came home from the office some nights later that she and Edward had been at it. After him, I knew she wanted fucking again, being aroused by the thought of two men having her close together. One night when her car was being serviced, he drove her home from work and I asked him in. He sat on the sofa beside my wife and I went into the kitchen to make them coffee. I was sure they'd been at it on the way home. I thought her lips looked soft and wet as if she'd sucked him off.

In the kitchen, ears cocked, I noticed their chatter had stopped. Peeking around the door I saw them kissing passionately, surprised at how erotic it was to see them. My prick stirred and I guessed that this was how wife-watchers got their kicks. I saw her hand had hold of his cock through his trousers, slowly rubbing it while he cupped her tits. They drew apart as I returned with the coffee, although I secretly hoped they would continue kissing and groping. 'Moira's told me you know all about us,' Edward said, surprising me. 'And you don't mind that we are lovers. She says you've got another woman yourself.'

'Something like that,' I admitted in my aroused state. He then asked if I could leave them, explaining that he was about to shag my wife. 'Darling, go to bed and I'll be up shortly,' Moira said, smiling. 'Be nice and I'll make it worth your while.' I went upstairs, my cock twitching, undressed, and then carefully went back downstairs.

Moira was naked, lying back on the sofa with her knees raised as Edward buried his face between her thighs. I stood by the door watching my wife having her cunt licked out by another guy, finding it a hell of a turn-on. Then, as she squirmed on his tongue, and he rose from between her legs, prick ready to penetrate, I thought what kind of dummy am I not to get my share first?

Bollock naked, and with my dick pointing to the ceiling, I strode in as both Moira and Edward looked at my hard-on. It was longer and thicker than Edward's I noted. Moira began to giggle, enjoying having her two men about to confront each other over her. She looked particularly desirable with her pointy tits bare and swollen cunt lips open and wet with her juice. 'Stand back and wait your turn, Eddie old chap,' I said. 'I'm going to fuck my wife while she's on offer. Thanks for working her up so well, by the way.'

Moira reached out, pulling me over her by the prick, then guiding it between her pussy lips. I heard her moan that she badly wanted to be fucked. 'Fuck me while Edward watches,' the horny cow said, and I loved her for it. 'Let's show him how to do it,' she added, and I warned her that I was going to screw her into a stupor, fuck the arse off her. Even with my first deep thrusts up her cranny, she shuddered and climaxed, the inside of her cunt so moist that my shaft worked in her like an oiled piston.

I'd never had such a hot juicy screw in my life. Below me I saw her face contort as she came time after time before I shot my wad into her with savage thrusts. Rolling off, leaving her gasping, I fingered her steaming pussy. 'Now you fuck her,' I said. Without hesitation, he turned her over on her belly and started to fuck her, thrusting between the upraised cheeks of her bottom.

Edward has been a welcome visitor since that night and soon after our threesome became a foursome. Alice from next door was invited to join us and quite hectic orgies take place weekly. What Moira wants she gets and right now that plenty of stuffing.

Timothy, Cambs

Doing the Double

Kidding myself that I haven't a jealous thought in my head, I agreed my wife could go off for a ten-day holiday in Majorca with the girls in her office. It was okay for them, of course, all were single and fancy-free, ripe for a holiday fuck with some lager lout or a Spanish waiter, or to enter a wet tee-shirt contest and show off their tits. Sally promised me she wasn't that kind of girl and would never forget she was my wife, but I detected a wicked gleam in her eye.

The lads at the pub thought I was taking too much of a risk. They joked that I should ask to see her topless snaps on the beach when she returned. Very funny, I'd say, but with an anxious feeling in the pit of my stomach. The night before she went, as if to thank me for letting her go, she did all the things I like. She let me fuck her big soft tits as well as her grasping cunnie; sucked me back to full erection and had a doggie-position shag as well. In the morning she mounted me for a hard fast ride and then left for her taxi to the airport.

The taxi contained four other giggling girls, all of them calling out to me that Sally wouldn't do anything that they wouldn't do, and they were good girls! Well, I consoled myself by eating out to save washing up, got a few porno videos from a mate who seemed to have an endless supply, and stuck out the first two days. On Saturday lunchtime, I was preparing to go to the local for one of their excellent bar meals, plus the odd beer, when the doorbell announced a visitor. Opening it, I saw my ma-in-law Netta.

She'd driven some fifty miles from her home to see if I was looking after myself. She said we were in the same boat as her husband, Tom, was also in Spain on a golfing holiday with some friends. I took her along to my local and we ate a hot delicious curry made by the Indian chef and drank lagers to cool our throats. Then we stayed in the pub until after three, my input of beer matched by Netta's several vodka-and-orange tipples.

The lads thought her lovely, buying her drink and mildly flirting with this very shapely older woman. On one of my visits to the toilet I was pressed to know who she was by a chap I barely knew, saying he admired my taste. Older women were more grateful and more experienced, he said, and my bit had gorgeous big tits and a fine rounded arse. I had noticed, I said, the thought of having Netta in the buff for nookie making me horny. I'd once read an adult magazine article on men who'd fucked both mother and daughter, entitled *Completing the Double*. I rather fancied doing that myself. I'd already had my wife, of course. Shagging her mum too would be a real result.

Arriving home, Netta said she had thoroughly enjoyed the outing, it being such a change from the bar of her husband's stuffy golf club. 'It was lovely and I could kiss you for it, Robert,' she said, no doubt light-headed with drink. Or was she, I pondered? 'I'll have that kiss if you're offering,' I said and opened my arms. I kissed her soft cheek, wondering if I would be rebuffed if I tried more. She pressed against me, her breasts flattening against my chest, her body fitting nicely into mine. Soon we were crotch to crotch with my stiff dick fitting snug in the fork of her thighs.

It was an embrace too far for us, I guess, for my mouth sought hers and she was ready with a probing tongue to meet my kiss on even terms. We kissed long and fervently until forced to come up for air. 'Am I too old to turn you on?' she asked hoarsely. 'What do you think?' I asked, easing my cock, now a hard bar of flesh, up and down against her cunt mound. I told her she was the sexiest woman I knew and had longed to fuck her ever since her daughter had taken me home. 'Then you should have tried before now, Robert,' she moaned, obviously as steamed up as I was. 'Do fuck me, my darling. Do whatever you want with me. Talk dirty too, I've always liked that.'

We groped and kissed all the way upstairs and I took her to the bed I shared with her daughter. A standing cock has no conscience, it's true, and the same must go for a throbbing cunt in need of a prick. Neither of us thought of Sally as we stood apart and got out of our clothes. Naked, she looked glorious, full-fleshed and rounded, her teats big and heavy, fat spheres with rubbery nipples like big acorns. She sat on the edge of the bed with her legs spread and cupping the sides of her breasts in her hands, nodding encouragement to me.

I went to her and she kissed the knob of my dick, gave it a brief suck and then nursed it in the cleavage of her tits. 'You can fuck my titties, Robert,' she said, 'but you musn't come yet. I want that nice big prick up inside me, making *me* come. You will do that later, won't you? I mean fuck my cunt and make me come over and over.' I promised myself whatever I did, I'd somehow save myself from coming before this delightful mother-in-law had had her fill and come over and over as she wanted. First I also wanted to increase her fervour, make her randy as possible. She likes dirty talk, I thought, so I determined to give her some.

'You like a man playing with your tits, don't you?' I began. 'Sucking on those big nipples with a stiff prick working up between them. Your daughter can act like a slut when she's on heat. I can see now where she gets that from. I'll bet you've had a lot of big hard cocks in your time, haven't you?'

It had all been said spontaneously to arouse her, but the words evidently struck home. 'Oh, I love taking cocks, everywhere and anywhere,' she whined, working her shoulders so my prick moved up and down in her shaking cleavage. 'My Tom doesn't know how many men have fucked his wife over the years. I can't help it, I love the prick.' She looked up at me almost agonisingly. 'You'll fuck me too, won't you? Fuck me soon. Oh fuck me . . .'

I still wanted to give her a time to remember, so I knelt down between her legs and started licking and tonguing her pouting cunt, circling my tongue around a prominent clitoris. She lolled back on the bed with knees raised, her hands grasping my hair and moaning in ecstasy. Her gasps and sharp yelps told me she was on the brink of coming, so I looked down on her as I prepared to spear her. I saw her face contorted by lust, her great tits swaying on her chest, her cunt presented for the dick, gaping like a hungry mouth.

'Fuck me then, go on, do it! I heard her order, and again I just had to wonder about women. This one below me was outwardly the model of respectability, a school governor and church member, yet when on heat she was hornier than any paid whore. But why not?

By then my bollocks were aching to unload spunk

and so I went into her to the hilt, deep into a hot juicy cranny and began a steady rhythmic thrusting. I could barely decipher her mumblings as she seemed delirious with the pleasure of the cock inside her. 'Give it to me, balls and all!' she screamed.

Netta was indeed a marvellous screw, gyrating and jerking against me, very vocal and lewd in her commands. With her legs clamped about my waist, her orgasmic spasms seemingly unending and my own climax near, I could hardly believe the good fortune that gave me the opportunity of fucking this highly-sexed older woman who also happened to be my wife's mother. Right then, I was glad Sally was in Spain out of the way and I didn't care who she was fucking. At that moment I was shooting my hot cream deep into her mother!

We made love throughout the evening and Netta decided she would stay the night. She stayed the whole weekend during which we did everything possible between consenting men and women. I think she remained naked the whole time on my insistence. We fucked in every room in the house, in the bath, up against the kitchen sink. When she finally left we agreed, while hugging and kissing frantically, that it would stop at that. We'd had our special time but as mother-in-law and son-in-law it was not right that we should continue.

That was easier said than done, of course. Meeting as we did at family gatherings it was hard to keep our hands off each other. Once, driving her back after a visit, we stopped and fucked along the back seat of my car. She'd deliberately said her car was in for a service so she could visit by bus and have me drive her home. Another risky session was when we had a quickie upstairs while my wife and father-in-law were downstairs watching television. We'd been unable to resist. I never did find out whether Sally had got her end away on that holiday. Ignorance, in this case, was bliss all round.

Robert, Salisbury

Bedtime Stories

Reading wife-watching experiences got me sexually excited by the thought of seeing another man making love to my wife. It was reinforced in my mind after we watched a blue video at the house of some friends. The main actor was a black man of huge proportions. Someone joked that it was obvious the actor had auditioned for the role and won by a length. I glanced at my wife and saw she wasn't joining in the laughter, her face was flushed and her gaze was intent on the screen.

That night in bed I went on about the sight of that huge black prick thrusting in and out of thc cunts of three women. While reminding Chloe about the length and girth of it, I knew she was sexually aroused by my talk and the memory. I pulled off her nightie and got her naked. Then I sucked her breasts and licked her cunt, which was absolutely soaked. As I mounted her and began to fuck her slowly, I told her I'd like to see that monster black dick penetrating her.

She responded more than usual, even muttering that I fuck her harder as I whispered lurid details of how that huge prick would fill her cunt. Responding feverishly to my delight, she was quickly brought to a shattering climax, and reaching an orgasm was not usual for her. After that, we found that making love took place with much more frequency, even four or five times a week. The reason for this, my woman said, was because I deliberately excited her with lewd talk, saying how much

I would enjoy watching another man fucking her.

I borrowed the video off my friend and we watched it over and over. Chloe admitted she would like a penis of such big proportions inside her and that the thought of being fucked by a well-endowed man was now strangely attractive to her. She blamed me for this, but still we enjoyed sex as never before, with me describing how it would be with her mounted by a stranger while I watched. As fate would have it, around that time when I had a horny wife for the first time, our next door neighbours took in a lodger. Hector was black, very good-looking and muscular. From Nigeria, he was in Britain on a three-month computer course at the local tech.

I got talking to him and found his hosts were not sports fans. So Hector came to our place whenever football was on the telly. He was polite with my wife, so I gave up an initial hope that I'd get to watch the pair of them screwing. There were other Africans in town on the same course. I was sure some of them wouldn't have turned down a fuck with my curvy 30-year-old wife. Then, on the evening before the day Hector was to fly home, he looked into our house to say goodbye.

I shook hands with the lad, wishing him luck. Then, standing back to let my wife say her farewell, I noticed she seemed upset. With a look at me as if to say, 'I can't help myself,' she put her arms around his neck and pulled his lips towards hers. Hector was hesitant for a moment but, with me giving him the nod that it was okay, he kissed her. At first it was a gentle embrace, but soon to my utter amazement they were snogging like horny teenagers, with mouths open and tongues probing. Their hands were all over each other's bodies: his squeezing and fondling Chloe's tits and her hand groping at the big bulge in his crotch.

It was obvious to me that my wife wanted this young black man. She turned to me sobbing that she didn't care what I thought and led him up the stairs to our bedroom. I'd long fantasised about seeing her get fucked but now it was about to happen I wasn't too sure. I followed them up to the bedroom minutes later, unsure whether I could face witnessing her taking Hector's dick. I found them already naked with his cock rearing magnificently as he caressed Chloe's swollen tits. Then, after long moments of kissing her cunt, he lowered her across the bed and positioned his solid body between the fork of her open thighs.

I saw her guide his stander to the mouth of her cunt. With one powerful thrust his prick slid deep inside her, making her gasp and arch her back. His cock was pumping away inside her when I heard her scream she was coming. Grabbing at his flailing black buttocks, she went into spasms and climaxed just as he gave a loud groan and shivered uncontrollably. I could imagine his spurting cock deep inside her, filling the recess with his hot spunk.

As I watched I forgot it was my wife being rogered so magnificently. And they ignored me as they set about it again, slaking their thirst for each other's bodies without inhibition. After young Hector had left, I sat on the bed beside Chloe, where she lay prostrate from being fucked to a frazzle by the black lad. I congratulated her on putting up a great show. 'No faking there,' I said, 'not by the way your arse was jerking when you came and the wild look in your eyes.'

'Pity you left it until Hector's last evening to get fucked,' I said, thinking of the watching I'd missed and the pictures I could have taken. It wasn't until months later that Chloe admitted that she and Hector had been fucking from soon after his arriving in England. That's what I got for making her randy with my bedtime stories!

Cedric, Belfast

The Best Chest

My mate Steve and I work for an auctioneer. Actually, I'm trying to get into the antiques business and, while learning the trade, I drive my boss's van. When people call to say they have stuff to go for sale at auction, with hunky (if thick) Steve to help me, I collect their furniture to take up to the sale room. It was on one hot afternoon last summer that I called at a lone ivy-covered house in the country to pick up a Victorian sideboard. Steve stayed in the van reading his girlie mag while I knocked repeatedly at the front porch door.

Getting no answer I walked around the back of the house and found an extensive garden. By the back door I saw a pair of muddy boots and a cane basket with gardening gloves and small tools. I guessed my knocking had not been answered because the lady of the house had been gardening and now she had gone indoors just as I'd come round the back. Nearby was a kitchen window and I looked in. I stopped in my tracks as I came face to face with a woman having a good sluice at the kitchen sink.

No doubt she was hot and sweaty from work outside in the afternoon sun, but she was naked from the waist up. Her head was lowered as she splashed water over her arms and breasts and at first she did not see me. Of course I should have turned away, but I stood openly admiring as big a pair of tits as I'd seen. Being a young chap, it was the tits of girls my own age that I was used to. These facing me, with a lovely pendulous swing forward as she bent over the sink, were ample beauties, heavy with mass and weight, roundly fleshed with thick dark brown nipples. 'Lady, you got the tits', I murmured to myself, awestruck by the superb shape and size of such knockers. Then she glanced up and saw me ogling.

I'm certain I was the more shocked and embarrassed. She shook her head at me as if indicating I was staring, but she didn't rush to cover her enormous teats. Reaching for a towel and dabbing herself dry, with her free hand she pushed open the window and asked who I was. When I said I'd come for the sideboard, she let me in the back door. As we stood in the kitchen she dried her tits, seemingly unconcerned I couldn't keep my eyes off her magnificent twin mounds.

She was as tall as me, with a slender figure that made her huge breasts seem all the bigger. I guessed she was over forty, really attractive with a handsome face and dark brown hair. 'You're staring,' she teased me as she prepared to lead me to the sideboard. 'Young man, have you never seen a woman's breasts before?'

'None as good as yours,' I said automatically. If I'd thought about it I wouldn't have had the nerve to say such words. The sideboard was in a spare room with other bits of old furniture. She left me there and came back wearing a woollen cardigan with nothing underneath, as if it had been the first article of clothing she'd picked up to cover herself. The vee neck to the top button showed inches of creamy deep cleavage and the garment bulged with buttoned-up bare bosom. I went and got Steve out of the van to help me carry the sideboard out. 'Cor, did you see the tits on that lady?' he said. I said I had, the Full Monty bared, but he wouldn't believe me.

Returning to the house to get my delivery note signed, the woman asked if we'd like tea or beer? We were tilting the ice-cold cans to our lips when she pulled Steve's folded girlie mag out of his back pocket. Studying it, she held up a full-page colour picture of a girl with enormous breasts. 'You saw mine,' she teased me. 'Do you think I've got bigger ones than hers?'

Steve and I did double-takes, looking at each other in disbelief before looking at the woman expectantly. She was obviously enjoying keeping two randy young tit-men on the boil, well aware her outstanding chest had made an impact on us both. 'No contest, yours are bigger and nicer,' I said, feeling she expected an answer. There was no doubt she was enjoying the discussion and wanted it to continue, so I added, 'That girl in the magazine is just a picture. Yours are real, I saw them.'

'I wish I had,' Steve said, so wistfully that both the woman and myself burst out laughing. She was still chuckling over his forlorn expression as she unbuttoned the cardigan and let it fall open, her beautiful tits bobbing enticingly as she shook with mirth. 'I-I suppose a quick feel is out of the question?' Steve asked as if in a trance before such a thrusting, trembling display of flesh. In response she held one of his hands and took it to her right tit, clasping his palm over the curved flesh.

Not to be out of it, my cock rampant in my pants, I went on her left side and fondled that tit. She murmured sounds like *Ohh yesss*, and when Steve and I got the urge at the same time to kiss on her big brown succulent nipples, she swayed between us and moaned in her pleasure. Her hands went down to fumble at our crotches, squeezing our cocks through our jeans. I always took Steve to be the backward one, but it was he who asked if we could fuck her. Surprised at his taking the chance, I was glad he included me.

'You'd make me pregnant,' the woman said, but sounding disappointed all the same. 'Two horny young boys like you wouldn't want to stop once you came to the boil. I've got a husband. What would he think of that? If you need to come, why don't you rub up yourselves? Boys do, I know. I'll just watch.'

Glancing at each other, I knew Steve and I were in agreement. It seemed disgustingly erotic to wank ourselves off before a watching female, the more so because she'd suggested it. Besides, if she was not willing to allow us more, then it was better than nothing. She sat down on a kitchen chair and lolled back before us, her hands playing with her tits and pulling on her nipples while she told us to do as she said. Steve and I posed before her with our jeans and underpants pushed down past our knees. Rampant tools in hand we began stroking the trouser snake for her benefit as much as our own. It was obvious she was extremely aroused.

No more than we were making ourselves, of course. Aware the moment of climax was approaching for us both, she sat up with her shoulders straight and cupped her tits in her hands. 'Over me, over these,' she urged us. 'Shoot over my titties, boys. Soak them with your come.' She got what she wished, in moments our hot spunk shot out from our knobs in twin arcs, splattering the goo in her cleavage, up to her throat and dripping from each thick nipple. 'You'd better go now,' she said, once we had all recovered somewhat. 'My husband will be due home soon from work.'

She was not a sluttish type, just a decent woman who must have felt randy that afternoon, triggered off by me catching her bare-breasted. I put it down to a good fun experience that can happen in one's lifetime and was content to leave it at that. However, a few days later Steve didn't turn up for work. Next day he told the boss he'd felt unwell, but once sitting beside me in the van he grinned and said he'd called on the woman with the big tits. He'd phoned her in the morning, knowing her husband was off to work, and chatted her up until she'd agreed he could visit her.

Shows one should never accept people at face value. I was in my estimation the superior being, the best-looking one, due to achieve more while Steve was the oaf and had muscles for brains. In resentful sulks, I listened to his account of a day spent satisfying an older woman in about every way possible. He'd brought condoms, but these weren't necessary when he'd tit-fucked her or been sucked off in her generous mouth. When they had fucked he'd used up a packet of three before it was time to leave. An invitation to visit her again whenever the coast was clear had been extended, with the suggestion that Steve bring his pal along. No doubt the lady fancied a threesome.

We had many an afternoon before the affair ran its course, with Steve joining the army and me going away to college. The lone house in the country is now occupied by other people, and where the woman with the big tits is now I do not know. All I do know is that it was great for two young studs at the randiest time of their lives to meet such an obliging and uninhibited lady. There should be more like her.

Peter S., Lincolnshire

Victim of Love

I was always the wallflower, the plain girl who wasn't asked to dance, so I suppose it was inevitable I'd fall under the spell of the man who took my virginity and then dominated me body and soul. Let me share my experiences of being a sex slave and obediently serving a master over the past ten years.

When Richard met me through a dating agency, I was sure he would leave me on that first evening. He was a tall, good-looking journalist, a catch for any girl. I fell for him at once, scared he would dump me. Then, as we met over the first weeks, it became obvious to me he wanted a girl who would willingly obey all he demanded. By then I was besotted with him, addicted to his varied and uninhibited sex needs.

When he took me to a party with his friends, I would be ordered to dispense with my bra and knickers and wore only a thin blouse and mini-skirt. Being perhaps what one might call comely, my breasts are full and inclined to wobble. Braless, they shook like jellies when I was asked to dance, the nipples obvious through the thin silk material. As we stood in a group with drinks in our hands, Richard would blatantly fondle my bare bottom as if nobody was aware, while I blushed furiously. When ever I dared complain he would say he was ending our relationship. It ended with my begging him not to leave me, promising I would do anything for him and saying that I deserved to be punished.

What made me first suggest that I wasn't sure. Maybe I had a secret wish to receive punishment. I was already aware of the curious thrill I received in being submissive to the man, even to the point of cleaning his house and doing his washing and ironing, all the time tormented by the fear that he was seeing other women. My suggestion that I deserved punishing, though I'd done nothing more than stand up for myself, brought a smirk to his face and an order to go up to his bedroom and strip. He told me to wait for him bent forward over the edge of the bed, buttocks bared.

It seemed an eternity before he deigned to appear. On that first occasion, I waited fearfully for what I thought would be a mild spanking. Excitement as well as fear churned in my stomach. When Richard finally entered the room, he carried a whippy little cane that he swished noisily through the air.

He caned me until my bottom seemed on fire, but the heat also spread its glow to my sex. When he'd finished he made me kiss the cane and, although I felt humiliated as I did so, I realised that I had a need to be dominated in this way. That same night I had to submit to my master on my knees and beg him to make love to me. To fuck me, as he insisted I said. First, so that I would never question his authority, he insisted that I unzip him and suck his penis to hardness, then he made me resume my position across the bed. I was energetically taken from the rear position, for which I thanked him.

Eventually a pattern emerged: I would please him in whatever he asked while he consolidated his position as my lord and master. He had a lovely big penis and he used it to good effect on me when stiff. In turn I was made to pleasure him in various ways: by nursing his prick between by breasts, by sucking it and by stroking it to orgasm. I loved to lick and suck his cock. He'd order me to swallow his sperm after he had come in my mouth, then tell me to lick his flaccid stalk clean.

I obeyed each time by gently lapping with my tongue while massaging him to make him hard again. Then I would beg him to fuck me, longing for his prick to be rammed into my well-lubricated cunt. If I was too insistent about this and forgot my place, I would end up across his knee to be spanked. He understood my addiction perfectly and became merciless at using me for his own ends. I was ordered to bring myself to orgasm by masturbating before him, with my hand or sometimes a vibrator. When made to do this until climaxing, I was further humiliated myself by the scorn he poured on my head for self-pleasuring and abusing myself.

Sitting at home waiting to be serviced, hooked on the physical side of our relationship and the intensity of the orgasms he gave me, I was forbidden to contact him. So I waited, knowing that if I complained he might leave me for ever. If he telephoned I was ordered to tell him what I wanted him to do to me. I'd say I was desperate to be impaled on his prick, to feel it jerking inside me, filling me with his hot creamy spunk. 'Too bad I won't be coming round to see you then,' he'd sneer, 'you'll just have to play with yourself like the dirty girl you are.' If he felt inclined, he would remain on the phone listening to me using my fingers or a dildo.

At other times he would call out of the blue, ordering me to go to his house and pour drinks and serve snacks to his guests. I would be dressed in a frilly servant-girl's outfit, the top cut low and the skirt revealing my lower bottom cheeks. His friends knew how dependent I was on him and that he was mercilessly using me for his own ends. The women at these parties regarded me as a pathetic creature. One of them approached me to be her slave, promising that I would be dealt with severely to my full satisfaction.

But no one else has ever given me so much pleasure as my chosen master, even with the pain and humiliation I am made to suffer. He has made it plain we will never marry or live together; and he has never even promised to be faithful to me, although I must be to him. Sometimes it is weeks before I hear from him and I wait in an agony of ecstasy wondering when the next call will come. Whatever turns you on, they say. Being hopelessly in the power of my master is what I need. It's just my nature.

Barbara, Gloucester

The Sweet Taste of Success

After years of begging, I succeeded in getting my reluctant husband to perform cunnilingus on me – or lick me out as I prefer to say. My boyfriends used to do it and I loved their tongues probing my cunt. I used to pay them back by sucking their pricks and letting them come in my mouth. When I married Elliott he was still a virgin at twenty-four. He was shocked but highly delighted when on our honeymoon I sucked him off. He couldn't believe his luck!

So he encouraged me to give him head, moaning his abject pleasure as I gobbled and chewed his stalk. It was what I loved myself, of course, but I soon found I could wheedle anything out of Elliott by pleasing him so. Short of nothing: money, clothes, holidays, I'd wake him at night by sucking his dick, or go under the table when at his evening meal and have him in his throes as I sucked on his stalk. Heck, he thought himself the luckiest husband in the world, the only one with a wife who would do such a thing as have a prick in her mouth. He even told me he wondered what his mother would think if she should ever find out!

That was all very well, but I was missing out. I longed for my pussy to receive a good lapping and licking, something always guaranteed to give me multiple orgasmic spasms of the strongest kind. But where there's a will there's a way, even if Elliott regretfully refused my pleas, saying he found the idea of putting his mouth to my cunt repugnant. I blamed this on his mother's puritanical outlook and the way she'd instilled the idea of sex being dirty and wicked into her boy. Much as I didn't want to be unfaithful, in my need I allowed another woman to lick me out. She was good, I admit, but wanted me full-time as her lover and I'm no lesbian.

So Elliott had to be convinced beaver-hunting, muff-diving, going downstairs for lunch or whatever you care to call it, was good for the man as well as the woman. One thing Elliott loved as much as being sucked off was my breasts. Playing with them, kissing and most of all sucking on my nipples could keep him on a high for hours. My tits being sensitive and responsive, this suited me as I even played with them myself and plucked my nipples when I felt like masturbating. Elliott liked to be mothered, cuddled in my arms as he suckled me hungrily, petted and cooed at like a baby. We did nothing so outlandish as my putting him in nappies and baby clothes, but I wondered if he'd let me if I suggested that.

So, knowing his great love of sucking my breasts, I purposely wetted them one night with the musky juice of my vaginal lubrication. I went to bed first and before he joined me I fingered myself until really moist with arousal. With my fingers quite slippery with pungent oil from inside my pussy, I smeared the sticky secretions over both nipples quite liberally and could smell the strong scent. The same smell, I should add, that men loved when nose-deep into giving me a good tonguing. It was worth a try.

I told him not to wear his pyjamas, which always meant he was in for a sexual session. On joining me in bed I nursed him in my arms and directed a thick nipple to his lips. He began to suck on me noisily as usual, but there was something extra about the pleasurable sounds he made, like he was finding me especially tasty. As he suckled each breast in turn, I kept slipping a finger inside my puss and continued wetting my nipples. Suddenly, he gave a loud groan and helplessly shot his load over my stomach. Lying beside me gasping, he said he'd loved the taste of my nipples. What had I done?

In answer, I threw back the duvet, lying with my legs spread and my hand on my cunt. Elliott sat up, puzzled. I slipped a finger inside myself and began to masturbate before him. Already aroused by his ardent nipple-sucking and through playing with myself, I soon began to moan softly and contort my lower body. What man wouldn't get a kick watching a woman writhe as she masturbated? My husband was no exception. I could see by his face that he was turned on.

I brought out the two fingers from my very moist slit and rubbed them over my nipples. 'That's where the taste you liked so much came from, dear,' I informed him huskily. I then held my hand before his face and invited him to suck my wet fingers. He eagerly took them in his mouth and began sucking them clean. I wet them with my juices again and he continued to lick and suck them greedily. From lying prone beside him, a glance down showed me he was mightily rampant again despite climaxing not long before. Drawing my fingers from his mouth again, I used them to part the lips of my throbbing sex and tilted my pelvis in invitation for a licking-out.

'You love my taste and this is where it's at,' I told him. I saw him nod as if thrilled by the suggestion, then he buried his face between my thighs. In seconds, such was my response, I had the most explosive climax I'd ever experienced. Bucking into his face as he tongued me with a will, I shuddered continuously and lost count of my orgasms. Then, Elliott mounted me and rode me hard. I heard him calling me names like dirty bitch, nympho, slut as he lunged into me, words no doubt he'd wanted to use but had been too shy. Now the heightened passion he felt allowed anything and in return I urged him loudly to fuck me.

Once we had recovered, we debated the night's unusual bout and agreed it had been the best thing to happen in our quiet marriage. If we regret the wasted years, we have also decided to make up for lost time. For instance, while out visiting his mother recently, Elliott fucked me in the porch and I'm sure because his strict mum was just yards away we both found it wickedly arousing. The sixty-nine position, where I can suck off Elliott while he does the same for me, is also a firm and regular favourite of ours. We hope this letter encourages those not enjoying every possible aspect of their marital sex lives, to be open and honest with each other about their desires.

E. and M.B., Fife

Sauce for the Goose

My fiancé seemed to want to continue living as an unattached Jack-the-Lad. He announced he was going on holiday without me, just with his mates. I did really love him and didn't want him to go. I'd heard about Spanish holidays with girls, even nice ones, willing to have sex with boys on a first date. That was right up his alley, I knew. He was known as a one for the girls, including married women and other blokes' girlfriends. He was good-looking, charming and funny, which was why I fell for him. He was also very well hung with an 8-inch penis. I would miss that too while he was away.

Much as I adored Barry, how could I trust him? He was always chatting up other women. At last New Year's Eve party, I went into the kitchen to get a pack of lager from the fridge and caught him kissing my mother – and it wasn't just a peck on the cheek. Mum was a bit woozy from drink and he was taking advantage of her, I supposed, although she was clinging to him with their mouths fused. I forgave them but him going away with the lads was asking too much.

He'd been gone a few days when I thought I'd go to Spain myself, just to teach him a lesson. I booked into the same hotel and that first evening saw him leave with his mates and go to a disco. I went in and mingled with the dancers after a while, noting Barry had 'pulled' as they say, chatting up a blonde girl at the bar before leading her out to dance. Looking around, I saw a handsome blond chap so I walked up to him and asked him to dance.

Now I'm no dog, otherwise Barry would not have looked at me. I'm dark and pretty, with big sexy tits. I'd deliberately gone out bra-less and so they wobbled free under a thin white tee-shirt. If I may say so, my tits looked enormous and the boy I approached ogled them. The sight of them bulging under the thin cotton material seemed to mesmerise him. 'I'm getting a hard-on just looking at you,' the boy said, his accent sounding German. I felt like a tart, but I also felt good. Big as they are, I felt my tits swelling with arousal. The large darker circle of flesh around my projecting nipples was visible through the tee-shirt.

'Dance with me and rub that hard-on against my cunt,' I said brazenly. 'Play your cards right and you can get at the real thing.'

The boy grabbed me and soon was grinding his tool on my mound. Spotting my fiancé, I guided my partner close to where Barry was making out with his pick-up. As we bumped into them, I threw my arms around the German boy's neck and kissed him passionately. He responded immediately, his tongue probing my open mouth until we parted for air. Barry was standing as if struck dumb.

'Enjoying yourself without me?' I taunted him. 'This is good fun, isn't it? This lad I'm with says he wants me to show him my tits. He's got a hell of a hard-on. I think he wants to take me outside and use it.'

'You bitch, you followed me,' Barry said furiously while the girl he was with looked on amazed. 'Stop pushing your tits and fanny into that bloke. What do you think you are doing?'

'Having a ball on my own, same as you,' I retorted. Best of all was that Barry's mates were now surrounding us. They all knew we were engaged but while they reckoned Barry was within his rights to fuck others, as his fiancée I should remain faithful. Seeing me with the German boy was a great loss of face for Barry. To add to his anguish, I disappeared into the crowd with my partner, who took me outside, hopeful of having his way.

Actually I had no intention of paying Barry back that much. But strolling along with the boy, letting his hands fondle my breasts and allowing him lingering kisses really turned me on. Soon I found myself in an alley with his cock in my hand. It felt so smooth and inviting like a young boy's, that I knelt to give him a good sucking off. He asked if he could fuck me and, stepping out of my knicks and pulling up my skirt, I felt his fingers on my pussy. He found my clit and began to work me up. I told him to get on and fuck me, and directed his stiff smooth shaft between the lips of my cunt.

As he entered me I was surprised to find how wet I had become. With my back to the wall the boy shafted me more energetically than skilfully, but it was good. 'Keep fucking me, don't come yet,' I warned him, but I knew from his gasping and increased jerking into me that he was about to lose control. I thanked whoever was responsible for the pill as he shot a load right up my cunt, then with the vigour of youth continued fucking me with a rock-hard cock. Soon I was coming and I screamed at him to shag me, my bum bumping back against the wall as he shafted me.

Once I'd recovered, I gave him a kiss of thanks. He said it had been wonderful. It was his sixteenth birthday and his parents who were back in their hotel had let him out on his own as a treat. 'Did you know that was my first with a woman? Could you tell?' he asked, and I told him he'd been a very good lover, had made me come as well as any man. The boy shook my hand, of all things, and went off no doubt thinking that luck had befallen him that night. I realised I'd seduced a young boy for my own ends just to spite Barry. I did not even know the lad's name.

Back at the disco a wet tee-shirt contest was about to start. That was a good way to finish off the evening with Barry and his mates present, I decided, so stood in line with other girls keen to display their wares. When I was drenched with a bucket of warm water, my tits stood out like melons under the sodden cotton. When I stepped off the stage Barry was waiting for me.

'You've made your point,' he said. 'So let's call it quits from now. Just one thing – did that boy you picked up fuck you just now?'

'Of course not,' I said. But I don't think Barry believed me and I'm glad. What's sauce for the goose . . .

Josie, Liverpool

Just Good Neighbours

Even though I was glad to be free of the Wife from Hell, after a year I was missing regular nookie. Alimony payments kept me skint, leaving me permanently unable to wine and dine any prospective dates. My car was a necessity for getting to work, and at least I had a telly and video as I worked as service engineer. So I had free viewing, about my only single pleasure if you don't include a frequent wank.

My flat was a poor affair too, little more than a bedsit, so what worthwhile bird would visit there? Arriving home one evening, waiting for me in her dressing gown was the girl in the apartment upstairs. She'd arrived in town hoping to make it as a fashion designer, but so far had had to work in shops and burger bars. As hard-up as I was, paying extortionate rent just like me, she had no telephone and said it was her mother's birthday. Could she use mine?

We'd passed on the stairs, giving me the opportunity to look up and admire the round firmness of her sweet little arse. Her tits were small and pointy, her smile sweet and hair bobbed like she had cut it herself. One week a lazy postman had put her mail in my door, so I knew her name was Sarah. As I handed them to her next day she'd say no doubt they were rejections for jobs she'd applied for. Now I told her to talk to her mum as long as she liked. I went into the mini-kitchen to give her privacy, hearing her lie in her teeth to her mum that she was doing great and not to worry.

I put on the kettle and made coffee, sitting with her at the table on hard chairs because the flat didn't run to armchairs. She began to get a bit weepy, no doubt missing home. When I offered her my hankie, she looked at me with tear-filled eyes and said she was so lonely and unhappy. I held her to comfort her and she said she'd welcome a hug. 'I know you're alone too,' she said. I began to kiss her eyes and she tilted her face. 'Kiss me if you like,' she said. Our lips met and opened, our tongues met.

I guessed she was as horny as I was. We kissed until both of us were breathless and she'd allowed me a feel of her tits from the outside of her dressing gown. 'Let's get our clothes off,' I suggested and the pair of us stripped buck naked there in my room. She'd been to college so I guessed she was no virgin. I soon discovered she was no shy little girl either as she knelt down and took my hard prick in both hands. She fondled it for a moment and then sucked it between her sweet warm lips.

It felt great being suctioned between her tongue and the roof of her mouth. I began to move my pelvis, my tool sliding in and out of her pursed lips as I fucked her face. 'Suck me, suck me dry, Sarah,' I growled, my knees starting to buckle as I felt the surge of a climax building. Then I pushed her head away, despite her protesting she was enjoying it. 'It's Okay for you girls,' I told her. 'You can keep on fucking. I was on my way to shoot my load in your mouth. Much as I'd like that, I'd rather spurt it into your cunt.'

We rolled around on my bed, first me on top and then her straddling me, tempting my lips with the tips of her nipples as she rode my dick. I thrust my hard prick up into the fleshy folds of her dilated cunt channel as if I'd never fucked before. 'I'm going to *come*, fuck me harder now, ram it all up!' she squealed. Then she was sobbing out that she *was* coming, gyrating her tight little arse into my groin, her pointy tits flying as I increased my lift into her, humping and driving home the stalk she was impaled on.

Then the explosion happened, both of us out of our minds with lust. The thrill was sensational as I shot my load simultaneously with her jerking in the spasms of her orgasm.

It turned out that Sarah was just the kind of a girl I like. When her mum came to visit I was invited to tea and I discovered she an older version of her daughter. She told me she was worried about her girl, begging me to keep an eye on her. I promised that I would do my best to see no man took advantage of her. Well, I had to, didn't I?

Sarah's designs finally got her a job in a fashion house, and she also found a boyfriend of her own age. However, as a mere apprentice, the pay was little more than she got waitressing so she remained living in the flat above me. It's quite a boost to the ego when a pretty girl half your age comes in from a date with her boyfriend and ends up in your bed. The crafty little thing is hardly allowing him a feel of her tits, letting him think she is not that kind of girl. He'll have to marry her to get his end away. In the meantime, she's got me to fall back on.

Harvey, Leytonstone

Collecting the Rent

When my uncle died he left me a flat in London which was rented out. I went up to London to inspect it, making it part of a rare day out. To impress the tenants, I wore a smart dress and coat, had my hair done. I reckoned I was still an attractive woman, my figure being what you might call full but curving in all the right places. A knock on the door was answered by a young man in his pyjama bottoms and no top. I introduced myself as his new landlady and he let me in, saying his flatmate was still in bed. He soon appeared in his dressing gown.

The two lads told me they were musicians who played in clubs at night. We got on famously and they asked me to have lunch with them. For me it was fun being with two handsome young men in a nice restaurant. I drank the wine they pressed on me and basked in their attentions. Whether they were kidding or not I was flattered. Back in the apartment in the afternoon, all of us in high spirits, one put on some music and the other danced with me, holding me close. When he kissed me I responded eagerly.

The other young man then got up and joined in. We were linked in a threesome, both of them taking turns to kiss me until I was quite dizzy. 'Are you having me on?' I asked, saying I was old enough to be their mum.

'Wouldn't you like a couple of toyboys?' they replied. This was the kind of flirtatious banter they came out with while hugging me and kissing me in turn. Serious or not, for one unused to flattery and being kissed by young men, my excitement was real and my knees went weak. 'You're wicked but I can't stop you,' I said. 'What is it the pair of you want – as if I didn't know?'

'Carl says he'd love to see your big boobs, and I want to see all of you, Barbara,' replied the one called Buzz.

I suppose I should have said no but I let them take me into a bedroom. Nothing like it had ever happened to me before. I stood while the pair of them unzipped and unhooked me, removing my dress and everything else until I stared at myself stark naked in the wardrobe's long mirror. My breasts had never seemed bigger, huge spherical mounds that felt swollen, their dark brown nipples standing out against my pale skin.

As for below, the mass of wiry brown hair on my pussy mound couldn't conceal the slit. Buzz put his hand down there and I felt the moist lips gape and almost suck his fingers inside as he touched me up. This while Carl was caressing the cheeks of my bottom, his mouth sucking hard on a nipple. I wasn't sure exactly what they had in mind, but all kinds of naughty possibilities were racing through my own. I had two young lovers and two stiff cocks at my disposal, the thought was enough to make the pulse in my crotch beat faster. Buzz's fingers and Carl's lips, made me desperate to feel the touch of their bodies joined to mine. Quivering in anticipation, I begged one of them to fuck me.

Returning on the train that evening, I was in a world of my own recalling the hours spent with two lovers younger than my own sons. How I'd climaxed with Buzz's touch on my clitoris, his finger flicking the hard nub. And Carl's sucking on the stiff peaks of my nipples before lowering me across the bed, his tongue entering me with the bridge of his nose rubbing my clitty as he licked me out. I'd wished time would halt and they could go on arousing me. Before each had fucked me in turn, I'd actually kissed the tips of their erect cocks. Later I'd sucked them both until their hot cream was spurting into my mouth.

But before that I'd been ecstatically penetrated by both, so helplessly responsive that they'd been loud in their praise. 'She beats any young girl,' they'd said, teasingly asking how many men it took to satisfy me. When would I return? They wanted to know. They wanted more and swore they would remember the feel and taste of me.

Carl had fucked me first and during the bout I'd mounted him, riding hard with my breasts flailing. Within seconds I had him coming, his hips jerking. Then Buzz had placed me on my elbows and knees, bottom tilted up to take his big prick. His thrusts slow and tortuous, making me feel I was drowning in pure joy as he poked me to several lovely shattering comes.

In bed that evening, still aroused by the memory of my fling, I made advances to my husband. When we'd fucked, I cuddled him into me and told him of the afternoon's events, shrewd enough to know it was just the thing to excite him. I had to tell him every detail, both of us finding it highly arousing. It was more than enough to get him stoutly erect again and we had sex twice in a night for the first time in as long as I could remember. As for me, fucked so much inside of a day, my cunt slack and still throbbing pleasantly from all the attention, I'd never felt better.

My husband was eager that I visit London again –

and so was I. After another trip to the apartment, and another orgy with the ardent Buzz and Carl, I invited them down to spend the weekend with us beside the sea. When they came, I told the boys that my husband didn't mind about our sexual romps and the three of us performed for him. It's the only way to collect the rent!

Barbara, Devon

Among Our Souvenirs

Stanley and I were not getting on. Following our latest row, I was moving his stuff into the spare room when I got the shock of my life. At the bottom of his chest-of-drawers, I found a padded envelope and inside were a whole sheaf of nude photos. All of them were of him and Sharon, his big-titted ex-wife, in sexy poses. No doubt they'd been taken by a timing device, for Stan is a keen amateur photographer. Some of the things he was doing to her, and she to him, I wouldn't have thought people would do. Not decent folk.

When I thrust the evidence under his nose, he said it was *my* fault. That our sex life was so pathetic that he'd been forced to turn to his ex-wife. This only after he'd tried to kid me the pictures were taken while they were still married. But I knew Sharon was dark-haired then and had since dyed her hair blonde. This was proved because in the disgusting pictures her mass of public hair was thick and dark as opposed to the blonde hair on her head. 'So what,' Stan said as I pointed this out, 'that could have been you in those poses if you weren't such a bloody prude.'

He wanted to destroy the pictures, but I said that pleasure would be mine. However, I didn't burn them. I found I became strangely aroused looking at them, fascinated by the woman's breasts and hairy sex and what the pair of them were doing. I'd always refused to take Stan's prick in my mouth to suck him off, or let him lick out and tongue-fuck my cunt as he liked to call it. Seeing them both doing these things, I had to wonder what it would be like and got a surge of arousal as I imagined Stan licking me out down there. It was obvious his ex loved it. To my shame I masturbated to relieve my feelings.

Later, disgusted with myself, I phoned Sharon to tell her I was going to inform her new husband about the pics. 'Go ahead,' she said calmly. 'Who do you think took the pictures?' I dropped the phone, wondering if at times the trio would have a threesome, an act which, I hated to admit, sometimes featured in my fantasies. I went round to see the woman, certain she'd been lying about her husband being present when Stan was fucking her. She let me in and was quite unruffled when I said I didn't believe her husband would let her be fucked by another man, let alone take pictures of it.

'You poor cow,' she said, shaking her head. 'You're a good-looking girl and Stan is nuts about you. But you keep the poor sod panting for a shag when he needs it. You're missing out on having a good time. Stan has a bigger prick than my husband and knows how to use it on a woman. He can fuck me any time, with my husband watching or not. Just look at these. See what you're missing.'

The pictures she showed me were of Stan, herself and another man, all naked on the bed and both men servicing her. She was being fucked, licked and fondled. In some of the scenes, she was lolling back using a large vibrating dildo to bring herself off. From the expression on her face it was obvious the dummy prick was doing the necessary. She watched my face as I studied the photo. 'That fascinates you, doesn't it? Have you never used a sex toy of any kind to give you multiple comes? You don't know what you're missing.'

I couldn't disguise my trembling and did not resist when Sharon took me in her arms to comfort me. At least, I thought it was meant to comfort me but, when she used a hand to cup my breast and pressed her lips to my neck, I knew the bitch intended to seduce me. 'Let yourself go for once,' she said salaciously. 'Have you never made love to a woman?'

Right there in her living room, in broad daylight, Sharon skilfully manoeuvred me out of my clothes and her own until we were both nude. The large breasts and pubic forest of hair that had intrigued me in the photographs were now on show. I was quivering with excitement as my fingertips brushed over her pussy lips. She closed her eyes as I sought a big nipple with my mouth and wormed a finger into her moist cunt. She made no move to stop me.

Instead she murmured how nice it was and guided me to the nearby couch. There we fell among the cushions and kissed madly, our breasts and cunnies pressed together. There was no way I could keep my legs together as she sought to get between them, rubbing her naked pussy hard against mine and making the same jerking movements like a man fucking. In response, I clamped my mouth to hers with my tongue probing, wrapping my legs around her back and thrusting back to match her strokes. Then I came and begged her to continue fucking me, which is more than a man can do after coming.

We were really in the throes when the living room door opened and Sharon's husband Ray walked in with my husband Stan. Startled as I was, Sharon held me down and continued riding me, while Ray and Stan approached. They looked down at us with lust in their eyes and began to strip off their clothes. 'You've been wrong about your Mary,' Ray said, speaking to Stan. 'She doesn't look such an ice-cold bitch lying there under Sharon. I've always fancied fucking Mary myself.'

'You'd better give her one then,' I heard Stan laugh. Both men had had drink, I could tell, but were merry more than tipsy. It had not affected their ability to get rigid erections, both of them standing naked with big cocks rearing. 'You go ahead and fuck her,' Stan said. 'I'll screw your Sharon and then we can change over.'

With that, he gave Sharon a good smart smack on her upraised bum and lifted her off me, dumping her on the carpet beside the couch. As I began to protest, Ray was on me and between my spread legs, splitting me with one well-directed thrust. His iron-hard stalk began driving into my soaking quim like a relentless piston, in moments making me rear up my body to his. I groaned, forgot to protest and even urged him on, feeling his girth plunging deeper and deeper with every thrust. 'Fuck me harder,' I ordered him. Twisting my head, looking over the edge of the couch, I saw my randy husband doing Sharon on the floor, her cries and grunts proof he was giving her the business.

By the time we went home later that evening, Stan had fucked me while Sharon and Ray watched and took instant photos of the scene. When I looked at them later, I wondered how and why I'd let things go so far. Then I realised. For once I'd really let my hair down. It had been great. Stan agreed when I told him. I felt like a tart and a slut, but it felt good.

Our visits to Ray and Sharon's have continued and

we've built up quite a photo album. I've also moved his stuff back.

Mary, Birmingham

More Thrilling Fiction from Headline Delta

UNDERCOVER

FELICE ASH

Alexa is the twin with a lust for life. Gorgeous, redheaded and irresistible, she has an appetite for sex it takes a string of lovers to satisfy. And, in her work as a private investigator, she'll go to any lengths to get what she wants.

Jess couldn't be more different from her identical twin and her life is going nowhere fast. Shy and inhibited, she can't remember when she last had a good time – in or out of bed.

So when Alexa suggests that her sister take her place while she works undercover, Jess is desperate enough to agree. She soon finds out there's more to it than wearing her sister's clothes – particularly when Alexa's lovers are determined to take them off . . .

FICTION / EROTICA 0 7472 4499 5

More Erotic Fiction from Headline Delta

Confessions

Maria Caprio

Tales of seduction

Zena and Jean-Paul are a sophisticated couple and they have a sophisticated way of keeping the fire of passion burning in their marriage. They play a game called Confessions. They tell each other true tales of seduction from their past – and also, if all goes to plan, from their future.

They agree to part for ten days. To roam Europe separately in search of sexual adventures, the more exotic, the more bizarre the better. To gather confessions. And then to meet up to share the fruits of their experiences. To confess . . .